DREAMALITE

Power Crystal

Once a Star Darling has granted her first wish
and returns to Starland, she receives a very
special treasure—a beautiful Power Crystal.

BRACELETS

Wish Pendant

A Wish Pendant is a powerful accessory worn
by a Star Darling. On Wishworld, it helps
her identify her Wisher and stores the
ever-important wish energy.

Piper's Perfect Dream

Piper's Perfect Dream

Shana Muldoon Zappa and Ahmet Zappa

with Zelda Rose

Disney Press

Los Angeles • New York

Copyright © 2016 by Shana Muldoon Zappa and Ahmet Zappa
Artwork © 2016 Disney Enterprises, Inc.

For information address Disney Press,
1101 Flower Street, Glendale, California 91201.

Printed in the United States of America
Reinforced Binding
First Paperback Edition, March 2016
1 3 5 7 9 10 8 6 4 2

FAC-025438-16015

Library of Congress Control Number: 2015953974
ISBN 978-1-4847-1426-3

SUSTAINABLE
FORESTRY
INITIATIVE

Certified Chain of Custody
Promoting Sustainable Forestry

www.sfiprogram.org
SFI-01054

The SFI label applies to the text stock

For more Disney Press fun, visit www.disneybooks.com

To our beautiful, sweet treasure,
Halo Violetta Zappa. You are pure light and joy
and our greatest inspiration. We love you soooo much.

May every step upon your path be blessed with positivity and
the understanding that you have the power within you to
manifest the most fulfilling life you can possibly imagine and
more. May you always remember that being different and true
to your highest self makes your inner star shine brighter.

Remember that you have the power of choice. . . . Choose thoughts
that feel good. Choose love and friendship that feed your spirit.
Choose actions for peace and nourishment. Choose boundaries
for the same. Choose what speaks to your creativity and unique
inner voice . . . what truly makes you happy. And always know
that no matter what you choose, you are unconditionally loved.

Look up to the stars and know you are never alone.
When in doubt, go within . . . the answers are all there.
Smiles light the world and laughter is the best medicine.
And NEVER EVER stop making wishes. . . .

Glow for it. . . .
Mommy and Daddy

And to everyone else here on "Wishworld":

May you realize that no matter where you are in life, no
matter what you look like or where you were born, you, too,
have the power within you to create the life of your dreams.
Through celebrating your own uniqueness, thinking positively,
and taking action, you can make your wishes come true.

Smile. The Star Darlings have your back.
We know how startastic you truly are.

Glow for it. . . .
Your friends,
Shana and Ahmet

Student Reports

NAME: Clover
BRIGHT DAY: January 5
FAVORITE COLOR: Purple
INTERESTS: Music, painting, studying
WISH: To be the best songwriter and DJ on Starland
WHY CHOSEN: Clover has great self-discipline, patience, and willpower. She is creative, responsible, dependable, and extremely loyal.
WATCH OUT FOR: Clover can be hard to read and she is reserved with those she doesn't know. She's afraid to take risks and can be a wisecracker at times.
SCHOOL YEAR: Second
POWER CRYSTAL: Panthera
WISH PENDANT: Barrette

NAME: Adora
BRIGHT DAY: February 14
FAVORITE COLOR: Sky blue
INTERESTS: Science, thinking about the future and how she can make it better
WISH: To be the top fashion designer on Starland
WHY CHOSEN: Adora is clever and popular and cares about the world around her. She's a deep thinker.
WATCH OUT FOR: Adora can have her head in the clouds and be thinking about other things.
SCHOOL YEAR: Third
POWER CRYSTAL: Azurica
WISH PENDANT: Watch

NAME: Piper
BRIGHT DAY: March 4
FAVORITE COLOR: Seafoam green
INTERESTS: Composing poetry and writing in her dream journal
WISH: To become the best version of herself she can possibly be and to share that by writing books
WHY CHOSEN: Piper is giving, kind, and sensitive. She is very intuitive and aware.
WATCH OUT FOR: Piper can be dreamy, absentminded, and wishy-washy. She can also be moody and easily swayed by the opinions of others.
SCHOOL YEAR: Second
POWER CRYSTAL: Dreamalite
WISH PENDANT: Bracelets

Starling Academy

NAME: Astra
BRIGHT DAY: April 9
FAVORITE COLOR: Red
INTERESTS: Individual sports
WISH: To be the best athlete on Starland—to win!
WHY CHOSEN: Astra is energetic, brave, clever, and confident. She has boundless energy and is always direct and to the point.
WATCH OUT FOR: Astra is sometimes cocky, self-centered, condescending, and brash.
SCHOOL YEAR: Second
POWER CRYSTAL: Quarrelite
WISH PENDANT: Wristbands

✦ • • ✦ • • ✦ • • ✦ • • ✦ • • ✦

NAME: Tessa
BRIGHT DAY: May 18
FAVORITE COLOR: Emerald green
INTERESTS: Food, flowers, love
WISH: To be successful enough that she can enjoy a life of luxury
WHY CHOSEN: Tessa is warm, charming, affectionate, trustworthy, and dependable. She has incredible drive and commitment.
WATCH OUT FOR: Tessa does not like to be rushed. She can be quite stubborn and often says no. She does not deal well with change and is prone to exaggeration. She can be easily sidetracked.
SCHOOL YEAR: Third
POWER CRYSTAL: Gossamer
WISH PENDANT: Brooch

✦ • • ✦ • • ✦ • • ✦ • • ✦ • • ✦

NAME: Gemma
BRIGHT DAY: June 2
FAVORITE COLOR: Orange
INTERESTS: Sharing her thoughts about almost anything
WISH: To be valued for her opinions on everything
WHY CHOSEN: Gemma is friendly, easygoing, funny, extroverted, and social. She knows a little bit about everything.
WATCH OUT FOR: Gemma talks—a lot—and can be a little too honest sometimes and offend others. She can have a short attention span and can be superficial.
SCHOOL YEAR: First
POWER CRYSTAL: Scatterite
WISH PENDANT: Earrings

Student Reports

NAME: Cassie
BRIGHT DAY: July 6
FAVORITE COLOR: White
INTERESTS: Reading, crafting
WISH: To be more independent and confident and less fearful
WHY CHOSEN: Cassie is extremely imaginative and artistic. She is a voracious reader and is loyal, caring, and a good friend. She is very intuitive.
WATCH OUT FOR: Cassie can be distrustful, jealous, moody, and brooding.
SCHOOL YEAR: First
POWER CRYSTAL: Lunalite
WISH PENDANT: Glasses

NAME: Leona
BRIGHT DAY: August 16
FAVORITE COLOR: Gold
INTERESTS: Acting, performing, dressing up
WISH: To be the most famous pop star on Starland
WHY CHOSEN: Leona is confident, hardworking, generous, open-minded, optimistic, caring, and a strong leader.
WATCH OUT FOR: Leona can be vain, opinionated, selfish, bossy, dramatic, and stubborn and is prone to losing her temper.
SCHOOL YEAR: Third
POWER CRYSTAL: Glisten paw
WISH PENDANT: Cuff

NAME: Vega
BRIGHT DAY: September 1
FAVORITE COLOR: Blue
INTERESTS: Exercising, analyzing, cleaning, solving puzzles
WISH: To be the top student at Starling Academy
WHY CHOSEN: Vega is reliable, observant, organized, and very focused.
WATCH OUT FOR: Vega can be opinionated about everything, and she can be fussy, uptight, critical, arrogant, and easily embarrassed.
SCHOOL YEAR: Second
POWER CRYSTAL: Queezle
WISH PENDANT: Belt

Starling Academy

NAME: Libby
BRIGHT DAY: October 12
FAVORITE COLOR: Pink
INTERESTS: Helping others, interior design, art, dancing
WISH: To give everyone what they need—both on Starland and through wish granting on Wishworld
WHY CHOSEN: Libby is generous, articulate, gracious, diplomatic, and kind.
WATCH OUT FOR: Libby can be indecisive and may try too hard to please everyone.
SCHOOL YEAR: First
POWER CRYSTAL: Charmelite
WISH PENDANT: Necklace

NAME: Scarlet
BRIGHT DAY: November 3
FAVORITE COLOR: Black
INTERESTS: Crystal climbing (and other extreme sports), magic, thrill seeking
WISH: To live on Wishworld
WHY CHOSEN: Scarlet is confident, intense, passionate, magnetic, curious, and very brave.
WATCH OUT FOR: Scarlet is a loner and can alienate others by being secretive, arrogant, stubborn, and jealous.
SCHOOL YEAR: Third
POWER CRYSTAL: Ravenstone
WISH PENDANT: Boots

NAME: Sage
BRIGHT DAY: December 1
FAVORITE COLOR: Lavender
INTERESTS: Travel, adventure, telling stories, nature, and philosophy
WISH: To become the best Wish-Granter Starland has ever seen
WHY CHOSEN: Sage is honest, adventurous, curious, optimistic, friendly, and relaxed.
WATCH OUT FOR: Sage has a quick temper! She can also be restless, irresponsible, and too trusting of others' opinions. She may jump to conclusions.
SCHOOL YEAR: First
POWER CRYSTAL: Lavenderite
WISH PENDANT: Necklace

Introduction

You take a deep breath, about to blow out the candles on your birthday cake. Clutching a coin in your fist, you get ready to toss it into the dancing waters of a fountain. You stare at your little brother as you each hold an end of a dried wishbone, about to pull. But what do you do first?

You make a wish, of course!

Ever wonder what happens right after you make that wish? *Not much*, you may be thinking.

Well, you'd be wrong.

Because something quite unexpected happens next. Each and every wish that is made becomes a glowing Wish Orb, invisible to the human eye. This undetectable orb zips through the air and into the heavens, on a one-way trip to the brightest star in the sky—a magnificent place called Starland. Starland is inhabited by Starlings, who look a lot like you and me, except they have a sparkly glow to their skin, and glittery hair in unique colors. And they have one more thing: magical powers. The Starlings use these powers to make good wishes come true, for when good wishes are granted, the result is positive energy. And the Starlings of Starland need this energy to keep their world running.

In case you are wondering, there are three kinds of Wish Orbs:

1) GOOD WISH ORBS. These wishes are positive and helpful and come from the heart. They are pretty and sparkly and are nurtured in climate-controlled Wish-Houses. They bloom into fantastical glowing orbs. When the time is right, they are presented to the appropriate Starling for wish fulfillment.

2) BAD WISH ORBS. These are for selfish, mean-spirited, or negative things. They don't sparkle

at all. They are immediately transported to a special containment center, as they are very dangerous and must not be granted.

3) IMPOSSIBLE WISH ORBS. These wishes are for things, like world peace and disease cures, that simply can't be granted by Starlings. These sparkle with an almost impossibly bright light and are taken to a special area of the Wish-House with tinted windows to contain the glare they produce. The hope is that one day they can be turned into good wishes the Starlings can help grant.

Starlings take their wish granting very seriously. There is a special school, called Starling Academy, that accepts only the best and brightest young Starling girls. They study hard for four years, and when they graduate, they are ready to start traveling to Wishworld to help grant wishes. For as long as anyone can remember, only graduates of wish-granting schools have ever been allowed to travel to Wishworld. But things have changed in a very big way.

Read on for the rest of the story. . . .

Prologue

STAR KINDNESS DAY GREETINGS

To: All My Darling Friends
From: Piper
Subject: Happy Star Kindness Day!

Happy Star Kindness Day,
A time to spread good cheer.
I'm sending this holo-text to say,
You glow, girls, all staryear.

With Love and Positivity,

Piper

P.S. Personal greetings to come!

To: Sage

From: Piper

Subject: Star Kindness Day Compliment

The first Star Darling to ride a star,

The first on a mission, traveling far.

You triumphed with your heart and glow,

Even gathering some energy flow.

To: Leona

From: Piper

Subject: Thinking of You on Star Kindness Day

The third to go to a faraway world,

You granted a wish, and energy swirled.

But on your way back to our land of light,

Your pendant turned as black as night.

"Why?" you asked, so sad and blue.

No one could answer, no one knew.

But do not fret, Leona dear,

You still rock, that much is clear.

To: Scarlet

From: Piper

Subject: Star Kindness Day Tidings

You had to leave the SD fold,

But you didn't give up, you were too bold.

You joined a mission with a regular Starling,

To prove you were a tried-and-true Darling.

But why did this happen at all?

Why did you take the fall?

Another question, another riddle,

But you stepped up to shine, no second fiddle.

You showed true grit

And even some wit.

My hat's off to you,

Glad you're back with the crew.

To: Cassie

From: Piper

Subject: An Affirmation on Star Kindness Day

Who knows what to do
When we're confused through and through?
You, sweet little Cassie, you always do.

And when you came back from a mission all spent?
The lights went out 100 percent.
But you stayed calm and cool and kept us together,
You figure things out, whenever, wherever.

CHAPTER
1

In her Little Dipper Dorm room, Piper finished her last holo-text. Then she swiped the screen on her Star-Zap to queue up all the messages. Star Kindness Day was the next day. A ceremony would be held in the morning, at precisely the moment the nighttime stars and the daytime sun could all be seen in the color-streaked sky.

It happened in the morning only once a staryear. And all over Starland, Starlings met in open areas to gaze at the sight. Light energy flowed. Everyone smiled. They exchanged positive messages then and for the rest of the starday—to loved ones, to strangers, and to everyone in between. Thoughtful compliments. Meaningful praise. Heartfelt affirmations. It was definitely Piper's favorite holiday.

At Starling Academy, all the students' messages would go out at once, while everyone gathered in the Star Quad before class. Piper checked her holo-texts one last time. She had her own holiday tradition: styling her compliments into poetry. What better way to get a loving message across, she felt, than using language that lifted the spirit, too?

That staryear, she'd worked especially hard on the poems. There had been many ups and downs for the Star Darlings. So much had happened already that year. All the SD missions—some successful, some not. So that day, of all days, Piper wanted her friends to feel good.

Finally pleased with her efforts, Piper tossed her Star-Zap onto a neat pile of pillows on the floor. She'd played around with poetry ideas for starweeks. *Should I use lightkus?* she'd wondered first.

That poetry originated from Lightku Isle, an isolated island with sandy, sparkling beaches, where the local Starlings spoke solely in those kinds of poems, spare and simple with only three lines of verse and seventeen syllables total.

How they managed this without even trying was a wonder to Piper. She herself strove for an effortless state of being on a stardaily basis. But the lightkus proved too difficult and limiting. So Piper went with sunnets, rhyming poems that could be any length and meter but needed to include a source of light.

The last staryear, when Piper was a relatively new first-year student, the holiday hadn't gone quite the way she'd wanted. She had labored long and hard over those holo-texts then, too. She'd wanted to reach out to every single student at Starling Academy. She'd wanted each student to feel good after reading her text; appreciated, even loved, she'd hoped.

She wrote one epic poem but it turned out to be so long and so serious no one bothered reading it. A hot flash of energy coursed through Piper, just remembering it. She'd felt like crying for stardays after.

This staryear, she was determined to get it right. She decided to focus only on students she knew well, and that meant mostly the Star Darlings. She tried to make the poems fun and light, too. Zippy, you might say. No one would think Piper particularly zippy, she knew. She tended to move slowly and unhurriedly, taking in her surroundings to be fully in the moment. But of course she had her own inner energy. And maybe this year she would manage to get that across in her poetry.

Piper leaned back against her soft pillow, closed her

eyes, and visualized each of her friends' smiling faces as they read her special words of encouragement. Well, maybe Scarlet and Leona wouldn't exactly be smiling. Even with her failed mission well in the past and band rehearsals on again, Leona was just beginning to bounce back.

As for Scarlet, she'd had an amazing kind of mission. After being booted out of the Star Darlings, she'd brought back wish energy and basically saved her substitute SD, Ophelia, in the bargain.

Still, it was hard to get a read on Scarlet. Piper wasn't sure what the older Starling was really thinking. One thing was crystal clear, though: Scarlet didn't like rooming with Leona. And Leona felt the same about Scarlet. Even when those poisonous flowers were removed from the girls' dorm rooms so they couldn't spread negativity, those two just couldn't get along.

Yes, there was a lot happening at the academy, and on Starland itself. That recent blackout after Cassie's mission, for instance, had thrown everyone off balance. Even the teachers weren't immune. Headmistress Lady Stella, usually so calm and serene—and an inspiration to Piper—seemed a little edgy. And the head of admissions, Lady Cordial, was stammering and hemming and hawing more than usual.

Now, more than ever, everyone needed to be centered and positive. So really, this was the perfect time for Star Kindness Day.

As Piper thought about everything, her stomach did an unexpected flip. Maybe she should send a positive poem to herself! She stretched to pick up her Star-Zap without lifting her head, then tapped the self-holo-text feature.

Piper's picture popped up in the corner of the screen: a serene, faraway expression on her face, thin seafoam-green eyebrows matching long straight seafoam-green hair, and big green eyes looking into the distance.

For the holo-photo, Piper had pulled her hair back in a ponytail. The ends reached well below her waist. Her expression was as calm as when she swam in Luminous Lake. And that was how she wanted to feel now. Centered and peaceful and wonderfully relaxed. What poem would bring her that mind-set?

Like the calm at the center of the storm . . . Piper began writing. Then she paused. What rhymed with *storm*? *The Little Dipper Dorm*, where first and second years lived!

Like the calm at the center of the storm,
Floating like a breeze through the Little Dipper Dorm.

Again, Piper stopped to think.

With dreams as your guiding light . . .

(Piper was a big believer in dreams holding life truths.)

Your thoughts bring deep insight.

It wasn't her best work, Piper knew. But it was getting late and she was growing tired. Piper liked to get the most sleep possible. After all, it was the startime of day when the body and mind regrouped and reconnected. Sure, she'd had her regular afternoon nap, but sometimes that just wasn't enough.

Piper focused on dimming the lights, and a starsec later, the white light faded to a soft, comforting shade of green, conducive to optimal rest. Piper shared a room with Vega, but each girl's side was uniquely her own.

Piper knew Vega was getting ready for bed, too. But it felt like she had her own secluded space, far removed from her roommate and the hustle and bustle of school. Everything was soft and fluid here. There wasn't one sharp edge in sight.

Piper's water bed was round; her pillows (dozens of them) were round. Her feathery ocean-blue throw rug and matching comforter were round. Even her leafy green plants were in pretty round bowls. And each one gave off a soothing scent that calmed and renewed her.

"Sleep tight, good night, don't let the moonbugs bite," Vega called out.

"Starry dreams," Piper replied softly. She heard Vega opening and closing drawers, neatening everything into well-organized groups, and stacking holo-books in her orderly way. Everyone had their own sleep rituals, Piper knew, and she did admire the way Vega kept her side neat. A place for everything, and everything in its place.

Piper reached to the floor, scooping up another pillow—this one had turquoise tassels and a pattern of swirls—and tucking it behind her head. Then she realized with a start she was still wearing her day clothes: a long sleeveless dress made from glimmerworm silk. It could, in fact, pass as a nightgown. Piper's day clothes weren't all that different from her night ones. But Piper believed in the mind-body connection—in this case, changing clothes to change her frame of mind.

Piper slipped on a satiny nightgown, with buttons as soft as glowmoss running from top to bottom. Then she misted the room with essence of dramboozle, a natural herb that promoted sweet dreams and comforting sleep. Next in her bedtime ritual came the choosing of the sleep mask. That night she sifted through her basket of masks, choosing one that pictured a stand of gloak trees.

It showed a wonderful balance of strength and beauty, Piper thought.

Finally, Piper picked up her latest dream diary. She wanted to replay her last dream—the one from her afternoon nap. Frequently, those dreams were her most vivid. At night Piper listened to class lectures while she slept, studying in the efficient Starling method. And sometimes the professors' voices blended with her dreams in an oddly disconcerting way.

Once, she felt on the verge of a mighty epiphany—a revelation about the meaning of light. *What is the meaning of light?* was a question that had plagued Starling scholars for hydrongs and hydrongs of years. And the answer was about to be revealed. To her!

But just when Piper's thoughts were closing in on it, her Astral Accounting teacher's voice had interrupted, monotonously intoning the number 1,792. And Piper felt sure that wasn't the right answer.

But that afternoon's dream proceeded without numbers or facts or formulas: Piper was floating through space, traveling past planets and stars, when a Wishling girl with bright shiny eyes and an eager expression grabbed her hand. Suddenly, the scene shifted to the Crystal Mountains, the most beautiful in all of Starland, just across the lake from Starling Academy. It was a sight

Piper looked at with pleasure every starday. But now she was climbing a mountain, still holding hands with the girl. As she led the way up a trail, the lulling sound of keytar music echoed everywhere, and she laughed with pleasure as a flutterfocus landed on her shoulder. Another flutterfocus settled on the shoulder of the girl.

"It looks like a butterfly!" the girl said, as delighted as Piper. "But sparkly!"

"And they bring luck!" Piper answered. But with each step the girls took, more and more flutterfocuses circled them. Now the creatures seemed angry, baring enormous sharp teeth. "What's going on?" the Wishling cried. She squeezed Piper's hand, beginning to panic.

"I don't know," Piper said, keeping her voice calm. "These aren't like flutterfocuses at all! They're usually quite gentle, like all animals here!" Maybe if she could say something, do something, the flutterfocuses would return to their sweet, normal ways. "Concentrate," Piper told herself, "concentrate. . . ."

Perhaps if they reached the plateau at the very top, edged with bright-colored bluebeezel flowers, the flutterfocuses would settle down.

Meanwhile, she held tight to the girl, pulling her up step by step. And finally, there was the peak, just within reach. She opened her mouth to tell the girl, "We're there," when a blinding light stopped her in her tracks.

"Oh, star apologies!" Vega had said, turning off the room light with a quick glance. Vega was very good at energy manipulation. But she wasn't very good at realizing when Piper was sleeping.

Thinking about it now, Piper wondered why the dream, which had begun so well, had turned so unpleasant. She didn't want to call it a nightmare. First of all, she'd dreamed it in the middle of the day! Second, Piper believed that even the scariest, darkest dreams held meaning and could bring enlightenment. Piper felt sure this dream meant something important.

A Wishling girl . . . a difficult journey filled with danger and decisions . . . It was obvious, Piper saw now.

"I'm going on the next Wish Mission," she said aloud. It would be a successful mission, too, since in her dream, she and the girl had reached the mountaintop. Her smile faded slightly. Well, they had just about reached the top.

"What's going on?" Vega asked groggily, hearing Piper's voice.

"Nothing," Piper said quickly. Practical Vega wasn't one to believe in premonitions or dream symbols.

Once, while Vega slept, Piper had tiptoed over to watch her face for signs of emotion as she dreamed. Vega had woken up and been totally creeped out to find Piper mere micronas away and staring. The girls generally got along, and they were friends—not best friends, but friends. And it helped for Piper to keep her sometimes strange insights to herself. She didn't want to upset the delicate balance.

Now, thinking about balance, she decided on a new bedtime visualization. She pictured a scale she'd seen in Wishling History class. It had a pan on each side, and when they were balanced, the pans were level. Adding weight to one would lift the other higher.

In her mind's eye, Piper placed a pebble first on one pan, then the other, again and again, so the scale moved up and down in a rhythm. Piper felt her head nodding in the same motion as she drifted off into another dream. . . .

As soon as the first glimmer of morning light landed on Piper's face, she opened her eyes. It was Star Kindness Day! She had a sense of expectation; something was about to happen.

She glanced at her Star-Zap. A holo-text was just coming through from Astra: LET'S ALL MEET AT THE RADIANT RECREATION CENTER BEFORE BREAKFAST.

Piper half groaned. She loved going to the rec center for meditation class, but she doubted Astra wanted them all to sit still and think deeply. Most likely, she wanted to organize everyone for an early-morning star ball game. Well, Piper could be a good sport, so she made her way to the center, only to find the place deserted.

Then Leona holo-texted: I'M AT THE BAND SHELL. AREN'T WE SUPPOSED TO HAVE A PRE-BREAKFAST BAND REHEARSAL, WITH AN SD AUDIENCE?

Immediately, the Star-Zap beeped again with a message from Cassie: NO! WE'RE SUPPOSED TO MEET AT LUMINOUS LIBRARY!

Not knowing what to do, Piper went to the band shell, then to the library, then searched across the quad for the Star Darlings. But everywhere she went turned out to be wrong. Her Star-Zap beeped again and again, with message after message, louder and louder each time, until Piper shut it off with a flick of her wrist and realized she'd just turned off her alarm.

It was another dream.

Piper quickly entered it into her dream diary. She'd have to analyze it more, but it seemed to focus on mixed-up communications—not a good sign. Frowning, she looked toward Vega's part of the room.

"Are you going to the Celestial Café?" she called out.

Vega looked at her strangely. "Of course. It's break-fast time."

"Just making sure," Piper said. "I still need to take a sparkle shower. So I'll see you there."

The sparkle shower made Piper's skin and hair glimmer brighter, and she felt its energy like a gentle boost of power. But the dream lingered, making her feel somehow off-kilter. She couldn't shake the feeling she'd show up at the cafeteria and everyone else would be having a special picnic breakfast at the orchard, or by the lake, or anywhere she wasn't.

By then, Piper was already late. No one would be concerned, though. Piper was frequently the last to arrive. She often needed to go back to her room to retrieve a forgotten item. But sometimes it was simply because she liked to take her time. Even now she paused to add a few more notes to her diary, while the dream was still fresh in her mind. It always helped to get everything down in writing, though she could usually remember details for at least a double starweek.

Even as a young Starling in Wee Constellation School, Piper could tell her mom specifics of her dreams, right down to what color socks she wore. Starmazingly, her mom sometimes wore the same color socks in her own dreams—and their actions often matched, too.

It had been hard to make friends growing up in the Gloom Flats; there weren't many girls Piper's age. The homes were spread so far apart it didn't make sense to have a Cosmic Transporter linking houses. So Piper had always felt an extra-special close connection to her mother.

When her granddad completed his Cycle of Life, Piper and her mom both dreamed that Piper and her older brother moved in with their grandmother on the other side of town. It seemed it was meant to be. Besides, her mom and dad were busy giving meditation workshops throughout Starland. It made sense for Piper and Finn to stay with their grandma. And Piper loved her grandmother's home, a mysterious old house floozels from everything, with a musty attic filled with odds and ends and a basement that echoed with eerie noises in the middle of the night. Piper found it all oddly comforting, even if the kids from school refused to visit. But now she had more classmates living on her floor than there were Starlings in all of Gloom Flats. And at least some of them—the Star Darlings—were waiting for her at the café.

A few starmins later, Piper breezed into the dining area and slid into a seat at the Star Darlings' table. To Piper's way of thinking, their table had the best spot, right by the floor-to-ceiling window overlooking the Crystal Mountains. The others smiled at Piper. But they were too excited about Star Kindness Day to stop chattering and say hello.

Smiling back, Piper placed her order with the Bot-Bot waiter: starcakes with whipped beam. It arrived a starmin or two later, even quicker than usual. Already, the holiday seemed starmendously special.

Sage actually bounced in her chair, her wavy lavender hair flying. "I can't believe I don't have Lighterature today," she said with a giggle. "I stayed up so late writing an essay, 'Long Stardays' Journey into Light.' And I didn't even have to!" She giggled again.

Across the table, Adora nodded and mumbled something about missing Wishful Thinking class. At least Piper thought she said Wishful Thinking. Maybe she was really asking for a dishful of plinking, the delicious striped fruit that bounced like a ball, since the Bot-Bot hovered by her chair. Adora went on to say more, but Piper didn't catch a word.

She'd probably gotten some sparkles in her ear from

showering. She shook her head, and a bit of green glitter fell out. There, that was better. She was about to ask Adora to repeat herself when Clover flung her arms around her shoulders. "Piper!" she exclaimed.

Really, everyone was over the moon about this holiday, Piper thought. She dug a fork into the starcakes, then turned to Leona, who was sitting next to her.

"I'm going to race through the rest of breakfast so I can be closer-than-close to the stage for the ceremony," she was saying. Then she languidly picked up her spoon and slowly dipped it into her bowl of Sparkle-O's.

Piper sighed. Leona was being sarcastic again. She probably thought she didn't deserve compliments. It was sad, really, since before her mission Leona had lived for them. Piper believed the old saying "Don't judge a Starling until you've walked a floozel in her shoes." But she had difficulty understanding Leona's need for attention. Piper preferred to blend into the background if she could, to observe and understand her surroundings.

Tessa took a big swig of juice, then looked at the glass quizzically. "That's odd. It looks like glorange juice, but it tastes just like—"

"Mooncheese," said Piper.

"No, moonberries," said Tessa.

On the other side of the table, Scarlet stood up.

"Wish I could stay and compare moonberries and glorange juice." She gave an exaggerated yawn. "But I have to get to the quad early for the ceremony." She pulled a drumstick from her back pocket and flipped it in the air. Then she shot a look at Leona. "I'm the opening act."

"What?" Leona called after her, but Scarlet was already skipping away.

All around them now, Starlings were scraping back their chairs and starting to leave. The cafeteria took on a charged atmosphere.

"Let's all go," Piper said.

Immediately, the Star Darlings jumped up to join the stream of students heading for the ceremony. Most walked in pairs, linking arms in the Starling way. Soon the grassy star-shaped quad was filled with students looking around expectantly.

Star Kindness Day was here at last!

CHAPTER
2

Piper felt the excitement almost as if it was a real, live being, pulsing with vitality. But she sensed an undercurrent of worry as well.

Piper knew what some were wondering: *Will I get as many compliments as everyone else? What if my teacher compliments all the other students in my class, but not me? What if no one I complimented compliments me back?*

The negative energy felt strongest to her left, where Vivica stood. She was a girl none of the Star Darlings liked. Piper would be surprised if anyone truly did. But still, she was sure to receive hydrongs of compliments, since most students were afraid of her.

Moving away from Vivica, Piper edged between

Cassie and Astra. Cassie turned to Piper with a questioning look.

"What do you want, Piper?"

"Nothing," said Piper. "Why do you ask?"

Cassie stared at her. "Because you tapped my shoulder."

"Wasn't me," said Piper.

"But—" Cassie began.

Then Astra burst out laughing.

"Oh, it was *you*," said Cassie. "How can I help you?"

Astra shook her head, still laughing.

Just then Lady Stella swept up to the stage, the long sleeves of her luminous gown trailing gently behind her, and both girls turned their attention to the headmistress.

There was something about Lady Stella so right and so true that sometimes Piper couldn't look at her directly. Her sparkly aura was too intense. Scarlet skipped up behind her and settled behind a large set of drums.

Without Lady Stella's saying a word, the crowd quieted.

"Star greetings, Starlings!" Lady Stella said in a low voice that somehow carried to the far reaches of the quad. "We are about to begin."

As she spoke, professors and administrators gathered

behind her, smiling at the girls. Lady Cordial stood to the side, nodding. But even that small movement seemed nervous. She always made Piper nervous, too. Idly, Piper wondered if Lady Cordial's stutter would disappear if she learned some relaxation techniques.

"I expect throughout the day there will be compliments and positive messages galore," Lady Stella continued.

"Messages galore? Is Lady Stella so sure?" Vega, standing in front of Piper, turned to whisper to her friends while gesturing at Vivica.

"So don't be concerned if right now," Lady Stella was saying, "you don't receive as many as you'd like. In all, the good feelings and sense of well-being should be powerful, and the positive energy will last and last."

"Now please set your Star-Zaps to sensor mode, to send your holo-texts at the exact end of Scarlet's drumroll."

Scarlet rapped out a complicated *tat-a-tat-tat*. Cheers rang out at the end as, at the same starsec, each and every Starling's Star-Zap lit up with messages.

Eagerly, Piper swiped the screen for holo-text number one. The words appeared in the air directly at eye level. It was from Scarlet: YOU CREEP ME OUT, STARLOONY.

Piper gasped softly and read it again: YOU CREEP ME OUT, STAR-LOONY. It hadn't changed.

A wave of emotion swept over Piper, and a tear trickled down her cheek. *Shrug it off, Piper,* she told herself. It was just Scarlet being Scarlet. She'd probably written much worse to the other Starlings.

Piper went on to read the next text. Surely this one would be better. WAKE UP AND SMELL THE ZING, DREAM GIRL, YOU DON'T HAVE A CLUE ABOUT THE FUTURE, PAST, OR PRESENT. That was from Clover. That couldn't be right. The texts were so negative it was alarming.

Just then Clover strode over and gave Piper a big hug. She wouldn't be doing that if she meant the text! Piper sighed, relieved, and waited for an explanation. Instead, Clover glared at her with the force of a moonium shooting stars. "Glad to know you think I have a closed mind"—she checked her Star-Zap—"plus I'm the shallowest Starling around." Clover frowned. "Is that because I grew up in a circus?"

"No! That wasn't from me!" Piper protested. "It doesn't even rhyme!" But Clover was already hurrying off in a huff.

Piper heard a sniffle and turned to see Vega holding back tears. Vega was always so rational. What kind of compliment would get her teary? Without saying a word, Vega turned her Star-Zap around so Piper could read it: PLEASE PACK UP YOUR PUZZLES SO WE CAN GO OUR SEPARATE WAYS.

"I said just the opposite!" Piper said. "Something about our paths always merging." And she had actually commended Clover for being open-minded. The compliments had been turned inside out.

"Have you always felt this way, or did it just hit you on Star Kindness Day?" Vega asked sarcastically.

"I don't feel that way at all!" Piper practically shouted. But Vega was already gone.

Not knowing what else to do, Piper read more of her holo-texts.

YOUR HEAD IS ALWAYS IN THE STARS.

YOU SNEAK UP ON PEOPLE IN SUCH AN ANNOYING WAY.

READ A FASHION HOLO-MAGAZINE AND GET SOME STYLE.

Each and every text was insulting.

Two girls in front of Piper began to argue. "How can you call me a dimwit? I shine in every class."

"I didn't say that," the other retorted. "But why did you say I can't lift a moonfeather with my wish energy manipulation skills?"

Their next words were lost as the entire quad erupted in shouts and negative energy.

Piper pressed toward the stage, to get closer to Lady Stella. Surely just seeing her would set Piper's mind at ease. But Lady Stella was wringing her hands, distraught. "What do you think is going on?" she asked Lady Cordial.

"This is s-s-s-starmendously s-s-s-s-strange!" Lady Cordial shook her head, confused.

This situation certainly isn't helping her stammer, Piper thought.

Lady Stella closed her eyes, apparently gathering her thoughts, then stepped to center stage. "Starlings!" she called, raising her arms high. At first, the students were so caught up in their Star-Zaps and confronting one another, they didn't notice.

"Starlings!" Lady Stella called, slightly louder. One by one, the students looked toward the stage.

"Star salutations for your attention. There is a major mistake here, a mix-up of the very worst kind. Do not pay attention to these messages. Stay calm and go to your next class. Star Kindness Day will be postponed until we have figured out the problem." She smiled reassuringly. "Don't worry. Everything will work out."

Piper breathed a sigh of relief. For a starsec, she had

panicked like the others. But if Lady Stella said everything would be fine, Piper believed it.

Slowly, students began to disperse, heading toward
Halo Hall for classes. Only Piper stood still, so only
Piper heard Lady Stella say to Lady Cordial, "First the
blackout, now this. Another wave of negative energy is
the last thing we need."

Piper's heart quickened. Was Lady Stella saying
there was more to this than a simple technological mix-
up? That there wasn't a simple fix?

It was too much to think about, especially since
Piper was still smarting from the insulting comments.
You couldn't just forget about those kinds of holo-texts,
Piper realized, no matter what Lady Stella had said.
She knew her friends didn't always want to hear about
dreams or premonitions. But did they really think she
was weird and creepy? And unfashionable!

Piper's feelings were hurt, and she felt a tingle of neg-
ative energy travel from her head to her toes. Suddenly,
Piper wanted to be alone. She made her way around the
Celestial Café to the ozziefruit orchard.

There wasn't much time till her first class. But
Dododay was the only starday that she didn't have Inner-
light Meditation, and she needed to take some time to

herself. Moving quickly, Piper cut through rows of pink-leaved trees to the far end, where a small garden was tucked away. There she settled in her favorite spot, under a glimmerwillow tree. Its branches hung from the top in such a way that they created a closed-off leafy room.

Sitting inside, Piper immediately felt better. The smell of the sweet glimmervines, the soft damp earth, and the quiet were just what she needed. She crossed her legs, placed her hands palm up on her knees, and took a deep breath. She closed her eyes, breathing deeply, concentrating on the air going in . . . going out. Her heart rate slowed. Her tense shoulders relaxed.

Suddenly, her Star-Zap buzzed. *Starf!* She'd forgotten to turn it off, neglecting the first rule of meditation: silence all communication devices for true peace.

Still, Piper couldn't help sneaking a peek at the screen. It was a holo-text from Vega: I'M IN WISH THEORY. WHERE ARE YOU, DEARIE?

Dearie! Piper had to smile. Clearly, Vega couldn't be mad if she called her that! Even better, she was checking on Piper, making sure everything was okay. Maybe she'd already gotten over the negative texts.

BE RIGHT THERE, Piper holo-texted back.

But of course Piper was still late. Professor Illumia

Wickes motioned for Piper to sit down with barely a glance.

Quietly, Piper slid next to Vega. "Star salutations for reminding me about class," she said in a low voice. Vega gave her a curt nod. Clearly, she was still upset about Piper's "compliment."

Piper turned back to Professor Illumia Wickes. The teacher often liked to lead rambling class discussions about the philosophy behind wishes. So being a few starmins late shouldn't really matter. Usually, students could just jump in at any point; Piper expected the usual interesting debate.

That day, though, Professor Wickes glared around the room and said, "We will be focusing on the math portion of wish theory."

Math portion? Piper didn't remember there being anything about that in the syllabus. Neither, it seemed, did anyone else.

The students looked confused. "Don't just sit there!" Professor Illumia Wickes snapped. "Set your Star-Zaps to record. You will be quizzed on the material. Tomorrow." She started tapping out a series of numbers on a holo-device, and they were projected in the air. Three hundred and forty moonium, fourteen thousand and ninety-one was the smallest.

Ooh, thought Piper. *She must have gotten some seriously negative holo-texts.*

"Now plug these numbers into the appropriate wish-granting formula. Remember, any authentic theorist takes into account the sum of thoughts—"

"And actions," said Piper.

"Go on," said the professor. "Think about the true meaning behind the numbers."

"It's not how long the numbers are, or how complicated. It's the equation that matters in the end. And how you use it," Piper finished.

"Yes, star salutations for reminding us all, Piper," said the professor.

She deleted the numbers with a flick of her wrist and words appeared in the air. "We need to remember, too, that Starlings alone cannot grant wishes. Wishers need to make their own dreams come true; our job is to guide them. Generally, Wishlings have trouble manifesting their desires—not only impossible wishes, such as world peace, but personal, manageable ones as well. We are there to help them . . . ah . . . see the light."

"Huh?" said a girl named Shareen, who wore her bright yellow hair plaited around her head. "What does that—"

"Mean?" Piper jumped in. *Really, this is a silly first-year question*, she thought. And students made fun of the Star Darlings for taking their extra class, thinking it was for slow learners!

"Basically, Wishlings need help," Piper said, using the tone a baby Starling reciting the alphabet would. She sounded sarcastic, she knew, but she couldn't quite control her voice. Usually, she was better at that, but after that morning's upheaval and her interrupted meditation, her emotions seemed to have gotten the better of her. "They first need to figure out they can, in fact, make their wishes come true, and then understand the ways to make it happen."

Professor Illumia Wickes nodded, then pushed her glasses up the bridge of her nose and walked around the room. "Can anyone think of an equation, a sum of two or more parts, that would result in the desired outcome?"

Half a dozen ideas popped immediately into Piper's head.

Vega raised her hand. "Thought plus action equals no subtraction," she said.

The professor frowned. "I think what Vega is saying is that a thought plus an action can lead to a wish coming true. But it might not be that—"

"Simple," Piper offered.

Vega glared at her. "Maybe add 'believing in yourself'

to the equation," Piper said, almost apologetically.

"How about filling in the blanks for this equation?" The teacher's words appeared in the air: FAITH + TRUST +

_____ + ACTION = SUCCESSFUL WISHES.

"Luck!" Shareen guessed.

Piper choked back a giggle. "How about patience?"

"Maybe a little bit of both," the teacher acknowledged, more to be kind to Shareen than anything else, Piper thought. "But definitely patience. Now, let's try another one." She wrote another equation:

_____ + FOCUS + POSITIVE THINKING = WISHES TAKING FORM.

"Luck?" Shareen said again.

At the very same moment, Piper answered, "Visualization. You should visualize the wish coming true and think positively for the best results." This was child's play for Piper.

A girl named Lucinda shook her head. "Why did you even say 'luck,' Shareen? Clearly, it wasn't right the first time. Why would it be now?"

"Humph!" Shareen narrowed her eyes at Lucinda. "You think I have the brain power of a glowfur, don't you?" She looked around the room. "Does anyone else think so, too?" The class began to buzz.

Piper felt her own negative emotions boil over. All

she wanted to do was continue with the class. Those equations were important! But everyone else was acting as silly as a bloombug during a full moon.

A holo-vision of Lady Stella suddenly materialized in the front of the classroom and everyone fell silent. "Star apologies, teachers and students, for this interruption," Lady Stella said. She was standing in her office, hands clasped calmly in front of her. She seemed composed, but there was still a crease of worry on her forehead.

"I'd like to update everyone on the Star Kindness Day situation." She paused. "Clearly, something went very wrong with your holo-text compliments. Indeed, the messages were most likely the opposite of what each writer intended to say. We cannot let this enmity and distrust continue. The messages have vanished, which is just as well. So I'd like to ask each student to rewrite her original compliments. Reading the true holo-words may set us on the path back to good fellowship. Continue with your studies, but remember the meaning behind Star Kindness Day." She nodded twice and disappeared.

For a moment, the room was quiet. Lady Stella's words carried weight. Piper thought that it could possibly be enough, that everyone would agree: the way to feel good again was to spread good feeling.

Then Shareen snorted. "Why bother?" She glared at

Lucinda. "It can happen all over again. And you know what? I bet those *are* everyone's true feelings, and that's why the whole thing happened."

The class exploded. "You do think I'm clumsy, so you never choose me for your star ball team!" "You weren't late that day when we were supposed to meet at the Lightning Lounge. You just didn't want to come!" "So I'm just the tagalong tail to your comet, with no mind of my own, huh?"

Professor Illumia Wickes shrugged and let everyone shout until the period ended.

"Class dismissed," she said wearily.

"Wait," said Shareen. "Is there still going to be a quiz tomorrow?"

From then on, the starday only got worse. In fact, Piper thought girls were getting angrier and meaner by the starmin, and each class was more out of control than the one before. Finally, Piper headed to Lady Stella's office for the special Star Darlings class, during last period.

Just ahead of Piper, Sage and Cassie were walking in together. But there was enough space to fit a Starcar between them.

Inside, Piper nodded to the girls who were already

there—Sage, Clover, Adora, and Leona—and sat down.

Loud voices caused them all to look toward the door.

Tessa and Gemma walked in, matching each other stride for stride, angry look for angry look. "You absolutely think I don't do my share of work at the farm," said Gemma.

"Oh, please," said Tessa. "Forget about it, Gemma. Enough is enough."

"No, really, just admit it," Gemma continued.

Right then the door slid open and Lady Stella swept in.

She stood in front of the room and smiled, seeming calmer than she had earlier. "I'm glad to see you all here, given the kind of starday we've had. I've decided to cancel the guest lecture and talk to you about what's been going on. It's very, very important for all students to get along, but it's imperative for the Star Darlings to regain positive—"

"Vibrations," finished Piper.

Lady Stella smiled. "I was going to say feelings, but that works, too. Now I'd like everyone to gather in a circle and hold hands. We will offer Star Kindness thoughts, face to face.

"Why don't you begin, Vega?" the headmistress said.

Vega frowned slightly, then nodded. She turned to Astra. "You're great at all sports. But most of all, I like to watch you play star ball."

Astra beamed. "Star salutations, Vega. And I think you are very organized and good at puzzles."

Lady Stella smiled encouragingly. "Yes, that is the way it's done. Continue, please."

Clover opened her mouth to go next. But a knock on the door interrupted the compliments. Lady Cordial stuck her head in.

"S-s-s-so wonderful to s-s-s-s-see everyone together after those horrid holo-texts this morning. Lady St-st-st-st-stella, I was hoping to observe the c-c-c-c-class today."

Lady Stella smiled at the awkward head of admissions. "Normally, I'd welcome you, Lady Cordial," she said gently. "I hope you realize that. But today is not the best startime. Another starday would be best."

Lady Cordial ducked her head, looking embarrassed, and began to edge away.

"By the way," Lady Stella added, "I obviously don't think you are disorganized."

"St-st-star s-s-s-salutations," Lady Cordial said, already halfway out the door. "And I don't think you're an ineffective leader."

"Understood," said Lady Stella as the door closed quietly. "Now let's go on with our exercise."

Everyone took turns giving and receiving compliments. And while the class ran longer than usual, the girls left feeling much better.

It's amazing how a little positivity can improve your outlook, Piper thought. She grinned at Leona. Who would have known Leona liked Piper's sleep masks so much she wanted to borrow some for a holo-vid she wanted to make with the band called "Star in Disguise"?

Libby whispered in Gemma's ear. Gemma nodded. "Hey!" said Libby as they all moved toward the door. "Is everyone up for a sleepover in our room tonight?"

It was rare for all twelve Star Darlings to get together outside the Celestial Café or SD class. "What a great idea," said Piper quickly. She knew what Libby was thinking: *We need time together, without any outside stresses, where we can be like any Starling Academy students, hanging out with friends.*

But the girls weren't really like other Starling Academy students. They had responsibilities and pressures no one else could imagine. When everyone agreed to go, Piper could only hope for the best.

CHAPTER
3

At lightfall, Piper was busily packing for the sleepover. "Let's see," she said, looking around. She wanted to take her dream diary, her toothlight, a few carefully selected pillows and sleep masks—in case anyone wanted to borrow one—and a star-shaped stone she'd found by Luminous Lake the first week of her first year at school. The stone was smooth and pleasing to hold. Whenever she slept somewhere new, Piper always took her "serenity stone." It made her feel better.

After she packed, she changed into her nightgown, because why wait? Then she tossed everything into a star sack, which started about the same size as a lunch bag but kept expanding the more it held. At the last moment, Piper threw in another pillow.

Finally, she took the Cosmic Transporter to Libby

and Gemma's room and arrived at the same starmin as a Bot-Bot delivering twelve snuggle sacks. Piper loved the sacks. The heavily quilted tubes immediately adjusted to a Starling's height and body shape, so they were starmendously comfy when you slipped inside. It was like sleeping on a soft field of glowmoss, even if you were on a hard floor.

"Welcome!" Libby said. Piper noted the skylight, letting in beams of starlight, and felt her spirits rise higher—even when she realized she'd left her toothlight behind.

Meanwhile, the girls rushed to claim their snuggle sacks and a spot on the floor to sleep.

"Wait, everyone," said Libby. "There's plenty of room!" Then she took out her keytar. "Let's start the sleepover with a sing-along."

"You mean everyone sings at the same time?" said Leona, horrified. "This isn't some starcamp bonfire, you know."

Libby played a few chords. "Just give it a chance, Leona."

The girls sat in a circle and sang old favorites, like "Moonbeams and Rainbows" and "Stars in Your Eyes," then new hits, like "Lighten Up" and "Lightning Strikes Twice."

Afterward, they told stories about their first days at the academy. Piper admitted she'd gotten so lost she'd had to call for help on her Star-Zap—not once, not twice, but almost a hydrong times. Sage confided with a giggle that it had taken her starweeks to finally read the Student Manual.

The talk faded to a comfortable silence when Gemma suggested they give each other spa treatments. "It's always fun to do nails, but look." She held up her hands. "Our old polish has really held up."

"It's true," Tessa agreed. "No one needs new manicures."

"Well, we can still do our hair." Libby moved aside some sacks to clear space in a corner. "Who wants to be my first customer?"

"Not me," said Leona, marching over and plopping down on a cushion. She picked up a bottle of glitter spray. "Can you use this to highlight my extra-golden streaks?"

"Let me do it," said Astra, walking over. She took the spray and spritzed it all over Leona's hair. Immediately, the yellow curls turned bright magenta.

"How do I—"

"Look?" Piper interrupted Leona, shaking her head. "Here." She handed Leona a small hand mirror.

Smiling, Leona angled the mirror for the best view. "What?" she spluttered, angry sparks flying. "Astra, how could you make a mistake like that?"

"Star apologies, Leona!" Astra said. "It's just temporary. It will wash out."

Leona hurried off, and Astra started fiddling with Piper's hair. But Piper slid out from under her hands. She liked her hair color just fine.

It was a fun evening. After some hairstyle judging, snacking on starmores, a moonfeather pillow fight, and several rounds of starades, Cassie pointed to their hostess, who was already sound asleep.

"Looks like it's time to hit the sack," she said.

Gemma picked up the starstick that Astra had brought with her, walked over to the snuggle sacks, and smacked one of them.

"Really?" said her sister.

Soon they were all comfortably settled in their sacks, arranged in a star shape, with their heads in the center.

"You know," said Cassie, sitting up. "Have you noticed that there hasn't been a Wish Mission in a while?" She paused. "No offense, but maybe it's been postponed because mine went so startacularly well. . . ."

"Really, Cassie?" said Astra, picking up a stuffed twinkelope and tossing it at her.

As expected, it hit Cassie right in the middle of her forehead. Everyone laughed, Sage the longest and loudest. Cassie scowled (but goodnaturedly) and lay back down.

"So who do you think will go next?" Piper asked dreamily. Of course, Piper was convinced she knew the answer: she would! Hadn't her dream said as much?

"I don't know," said Vega. "Who here is wishin' to take on the next mission?"

Suddenly, Piper sat up in her sack and grinned. "I know! Maybe we can make a mission happen faster with a visualization. Let's hold hands and visualize our Wish Orbs."

She thought Leona or Scarlet might snicker. Neither one was particularly into mental imagery. Instead, they—along with every other Star Darling—reached out their hands. Even Libby seemed to sense something in her sleep and stretched out her arms.

"Close your eyes and imagine our special Wish-Cavern," Piper began in a low voice. "See the remaining Wish Orbs. Smell the aroma—a little Starlandy, a little Wishworldly."

Sage sniffed the air and giggled.

"Each and every Wish Orb is glowing," Piper went on. She could sense the girls smiling. "Now look closely at just one. That's your Wish Orb. Watch it glow. Feel the intensity."

Piper's own Wish Orb glowed so strongly she felt its heat. Suddenly, she saw a rainbow of colors shoot from her orb and flow right into the center of the Star Darlings' circle like a fountain of sparkly hues.

All twelve Star Darlings sat up with a start. Their faces glowed with wonder. Piper gazed at her friends. "Did you see it, too?" she asked.

Tessa nodded. "It was beautiful. Like flareworks at the Festival of Illumination."

"And it started right in front of you, Piper!" Gemma added.

Piper snuggled deeper into her sack. All that powerful wish energy had come from *her* visualization . . . *her* Wish Orb had exploded with light and color. . . . She was definitely the next Star Darling to go on a mission.

But what else did it mean? If she succeeded in her mission, would she collect more energy than ever before? And if she failed? What then? The stakes were so high Piper's toes tingled. She reached for her stone and rubbed her thumb along its edge.

The visualization over, some girls still whispered about the burst of color and light. Others talked about the boys at the school across the lake. Vega tried to get everyone to play A Moonium Questions.

But Piper's eyes were closing. She took a deep, cleansing breath, enjoying the feeling of warmth and heaviness that was overtaking her. Within starsecs, she was fast asleep.

Piper was dreaming she was moving through a shadowy landscape. A dim shape moved with her—a Starling Piper couldn't make out, but a dark presence nonetheless. Piper could feel in every star inch of her being that this Starling could not be trusted. She tried to pull away from the Starling, but it was difficult. She pushed herself to run faster, to be stronger. But then she stumbled. And suddenly, she was falling . . . falling. . . .

Piper woke up, gasping. She could still see the Starling's indistinct form, feel the menace. The idea that someone was not the Starling he or she seemed was so powerful, and the dream was so frightening, that Piper was shaking.

And why was she on the floor? Nothing looked familiar. She shook harder.

"It's okay, Piper." A cool hand brushed her forehead.

"You had a bad dream. That's all. You're here with us, safe and sound."

Piper breathed easier. She was in Libby's room with the other Star Darlings, of course. She turned to Sage, who was crouching beside her, her lavender eyes filled with concern.

"Star apologies for waking you, Sage."

"You don't have to apologize. My little brothers wake me up all the time," she said with a laugh. "It's fine, Piper. You had a bad dream."

"Well, that's just it," Piper explained quietly. "I don't think it's just a bad dream. I think it meant something. Something important."

Next to them, Leona muttered in her sleep and smiled like she was modeling for a holo-photo.

"Let's go outside," Sage whispered, "so we can really talk." She looked toward the door and it opened without a sound.

Piper nodded, and the two crept quietly around the sleeping girls. They stepped onto the Cosmic Transporter and made their way outside, where the moon shone with a comforting yellow light and starlight illuminated the trees with a lovely brightness. The girls settled in a soft grassy spot and for a moment watched the flareflies buzz in looping circles.

"So can I tell you my dream?" Piper finally asked. "Sometimes it helps to talk."

"Of course," said Sage.

"It starts on the Wishworld Surveillance Deck. I'm waiting for a shooting star to take me to Wishworld when a shadow falls over me. It's a Starling, an evil one, but I can't tell who, and this cold, clammy feeling comes over me—"

Sage stifled a giggle.

Piper stopped talking.

Sage shook her head and said, "Go on, Piper. I'm really listening."

"Okay. So this Starling reaches out to me, but I run away, and I'm running faster and faster. I can't tell where I am now; all I see is shadows."

Sage giggled again. She waved at Piper to continue, but with every word Piper said, Sage laughed louder and longer.

Piper stood up to leave, brushing grass from her nightgown.

"Wait—" Sage choked out between giggles. But Piper had had enough. She turned on her heel. "Come on, Piper," Sage pleaded.

"Why don't you just laugh at me so hard and long you'll never have the wish energy to move a glimmerfeather, much less anything else?" Piper said. No one had stronger energy manipulation skills than Sage, and Piper knew it was her secret pride.

Sage sucked in her breath, finally silent.

Without another word, Piper strode into the dorm and back to Libby and Gemma's room. But outside their door, she realized she wouldn't be able to get in. The scanner would refuse her entrance. Only Libby and Gemma were allowed automatic entry. Piper groaned. She didn't want to disturb anyone. Just then she heard Sage's giggles floating through the air.

Well, at least Sage would be stuck outside, too.

Piper sighed. She didn't like having those negative thoughts. And she certainly hadn't wanted to lash out the way she had at Sage. But sometimes she couldn't help herself. Maybe that would change after her mission. Right then she felt like she was in limbo, just waiting to be chosen.

Back in her own room, lying on her water bed, Piper felt doubly worse. Of course she had overreacted to Sage's giggle fits. Sage was just trying to help. And she must have been overtired. If Piper had said anything, even good night, she would have collapsed with laughter. Piper understood. She was exhausted, too. She'd sleep late the next day, no matter what.

Sure enough, Piper slept so late the next morning that when she walked into the café, the rest of the Star Darlings were finishing their meal. As soon as they saw Piper, they stopped talking.

Quickly, Piper slid into the empty seat between Clover and Astra. "So what did I miss this morning?" She was trying for a cheerful tone, but the corners of her mouth turned down, and suddenly, she was afraid she might cry. Sage must have told all the Star Darlings how sarcastic Piper had been the night before. Clover hugged her, which made Piper feel better for a starsec— until Clover stood up and hugged a first year walking by, a girl Piper doubted Clover even knew.

Pointedly, Sage moved a cloth napkin through the air, then onto Piper's lap. "See, Piper?" she said lightly. "I haven't used all my wish energy laughing." She giggled loudly and clapped a hand over her mouth. "Sorry," she said.

Sage didn't sound angry at her, and Piper sighed with relief.

"I was a little star-crazed myself last night, Sage. The sleepover helped us connect. Let's try to hold on to that feeling."

Piper waved to a Bot-Bot waiter to take her order. She wasn't very hungry, and she still felt a little tired. Clearly, Libby did, too. At some point during breakfast, she had put her head on the table and dozed off.

"I'll just have a large cup of Zing," Piper told the Bot-Bot. *That should help*, she thought as it zoomed off.

Vega's eyes widened in shock. "I can't believe you're only having Zing. You know it's not the healthiest thing."

Piper nodded. "I know, I know. But I really need to wake up," she explained. Her stomach grumbled. "Where is that Bot-Bot waiter?" she said. "Maybe I will order something."

Astra handed her a plate of astromuffins. "Go ahead, Piper, take one," she said. "Tessa will be back in a minute, but she won't mind."

Piper bit into the soft muffin. "Hot! Hot!" she cried, waving a hand in front of her mouth.

"Oh, sorry," said Tessa, who had just returned to the table. "I slathered them in starpepper jelly to cover up the moonberry taste."

Luckily, a Bot-Bot waiter had just brought over Piper's Zing. Gratefully, she took a long, deep gulp. "What?" she sputtered, spraying the drink everywhere. "That's not Zing!"

Clover leaned over to take a tentative sip. She made a face. "It's hot-spring tonic. Nobody likes it except—"

"Astra!" Piper finished.

Astra burst out laughing. "Okay, okay, Piper. I switched our drinks." She passed over the real cup of Zing. "I thought it would be funny."

Sage giggled.

"See? Sage thinks so."

"Sage thinks everything—and everyone—is funny," Leona said.

Piper took a sip of Zing. Nothing had been making much sense lately. But Piper tuned everything out, took a few deep breaths, and felt her shoulders relax. It was still early. What better incentive was there to stay centered when her Wish Mission could begin at any moment?

CHAPTER
4

for Piper, the starday passed slowly and peacefully. She took a long quiet walk and an afternoon nap that stretched till dinnertime. Still, she had a slightly fidgety feeling, a sense that something was about to happen.

During Star Darlings class, Piper had trouble paying attention to their guest lecturer, Professor Eugenia Bright. Professor Eugenia Bright taught Wish Granting. She stressed the importance of understanding the emotions behind a wish. Normally, Piper hung on her every word. Now she forced herself to focus as Professor Bright said, "You need to be sensitive to your Wisher to pick up on feeling and—"

"Desire," Piper interrupted automatically. The other girls seemed distracted, too. Sage kept giggling to herself.

Cassie took a lot of holo-selfies. Once again, Libby had her head on her desk. The class seemed to go on and on.

But time did pass, and by lightfall, Piper was already in her nightgown, studying her holo-books.

Stars crossed, she'd get enough done that she wouldn't have to listen to lectures while she slept. She wanted to keep her mind open, ready to receive the next dream message. Still, interpreting dreams could be tricky.

One time, while Piper was living with her parents, her mom had dreamed their door scanner kept announcing, "Guest! Guest!" She thought they'd wind up having hydrongs of Starlings for dinner that night. So she'd asked Bot-Bots to deliver star sack after star sack of sparklecorn to serve. Unfortunately, the dream merely meant their scanner was broken. Piper had sparklecorn sandwiches, sparklecorn salads, and just plain sparklecorn for starweeks.

She still didn't like sparklecorn, after all those staryears! As Piper smiled to herself, her Star-Zap buzzed. Piper felt a tingle. Could this be it? Could this be her mission?

Of course, every time her Star-Zap had gone off lately, she had wondered the same thing. But this time it was different: SD WISH ORB IDENTIFIED, read the holo-text. PROCEED TO LADY STELLA'S OFFICE IMMEDIATELY.

Piper moved as if she was in a dream, as if the Cosmic Transporter wasn't real, as if Halo Hall was just in her mind. When she reached Lady Stella's office, she had no real memory of getting there. But apparently, she had gotten there quickly. Piper was the first to arrive.

"Oh, Piper." Lady Stella smiled, standing at the doorway and ushering her inside. "You could have taken a few starsecs to change." She gestured at Piper's clothes.

Piper looked down. She was still wearing her nightgown.

One by one, the other girls came through the door. Some looked sleepy. Some looked wide-awake. Scarlet skipped in, as if she was in Physical Energy class, ready to go.

Everyone sat at Lady Stella's round silver table. Starlight streamed through the large windows, flashing on the Star Darlings' sparkly skin. Each girl twinkled with energy—except for Libby, who snored lightly.

Lady Stella walked around the table and leaned down to place her hands on Libby's shoulders. "Libby," she said with a gentle tap, "you need to stay awake." She squeezed her shoulders lightly.

"I know," Libby said without opening her eyes. "I'm just so tired."

"Let's assume Libby is listening and continue with

our meeting," Lady Stella continued, pacing around the table. Each girl twisted in her seat to follow the headmistress's graceful movements.

Lady Stella sounded as calm as ever, Piper thought. But why didn't she just stop and speak to them from her usual spot? She held herself a little stiffly, too, as if she was trying to contain some nervous energy.

"Soon we will head down to the Wish-Cavern to see who will be going on the next Wish Mission," she said. "Please remember that we still haven't determined what happened to Leona's Wish Pendant. Although this will most likely not happen again, whoever is chosen for this mission should proceed with caution."

Up till then, Piper had just assumed it wouldn't happen again. Leona had had a scary trip home. Her star had stalled and Vega had had to pick her up along the way. But now Piper didn't feel so sure. Quickly, she pushed away the negative thoughts. She wanted to relish this part of being a Star Darling. The starhours before a mission were filled with anticipation and optimism, a time before anything went wrong.

And if Piper concentrated on this mission . . . really concentrated . . . if she kept thinking positive thoughts and stayed alert . . . the stars were the limit.

Lady Stella pressed a secret button in her desk

drawer. A hidden door slid open to reveal the passage to the Star Darlings' own Wish-Cavern.

Piper took a deep breath and pushed back her chair. Sage pulled Libby to her feet. "It's time to get serious," she said with a giggle. Gemma moved slowly, too. And when her sister told her to "hop to it," Gemma jumped on one foot all the way to the door.

Piper barely noticed. She paused to breathe deeply. Then she followed everyone down the winding stairs to the underground cavern.

Piper loved going around and around, down and down along the stairway, catching sight of bitbat creatures hanging by their feet. Maybe one day she'd try that pose for meditation. Being upside down would bring a new angle, a different way of looking at the world.

But those thoughts were fleeting, too. Piper's focus narrowed to one vision: riding a shooting star to Wishworld.

In the Star Darlings' Wish-Cavern, a deeply magical place underground, the glass ceiling looked out on the dazzling night sky. Piper could make out the planet Trilight, its three circling moons casting yellow, blue, and red light.

Everyone was silent as they gathered around the

grassy platform. Each time, the ceremony happened a little differently. *How will it be for me?* Piper wondered.

Trilight's moons beamed three different-colored rays directly into the cavern. They joined together just above the platform to create one startlingly white light. The platform opened silently and a Wish Orb floated into the spotlight.

To Piper, it seemed the orb glowed brighter than any she'd seen before. It reflected all the colors of the rainbow as it spun around the Star Darlings, swooping in front of each one. Piper closed her eyes, its image burned in her mind. She knew when her eyes opened, the orb would be directly in front of her, waiting.

And it was.

"The Wish Orb has chosen," Lady Stella announced. "Congratulations, Piper."

CHAPTER
5

Piper slept a deep dreamless sleep that night. She woke up late, feeling refreshed. She had special permission to skip classes. So she took her time choosing Wishling clothes from her Wishworld Outfit Selector. Then she went for a long, leisurely hover-canoe ride around the Serenity Islands. While she leaned back in her seat and let the boat drift, her Star-Zap buzzed. A picture flashed on-screen: her mother. She always knew when something big was happening in Piper's life.

Piper wished she could confide in her mother, tell her everything about the Star Darlings and their missions. For now, though, she had to keep it all inside.

"Hello, Mom," Piper said as a hologram of her

mother appeared. She wore loose, flowing clothes and sat with her legs crossed on a colorful starmat.

"Hello, Pippy," her mom replied. "I had a starmazing dream about you last night. . . ." Her mother spoke about travel and journeys, and Piper nodded at every sentence. By the time she finished the holo-call, lights were flashing in Halo Hall, indicating regular classes were over. Star Darlings class wasn't being held. Instead, everyone was meeting on the Wishworld Surveillance Deck—the takeoff spot for Wishworld—to wish her well.

"Hi, Piper," Astra said in a low voice as she and Piper arrived at the Flash Vertical Mover at the same time. "It's a big—"

"Starday for me, isn't it? Yes!" Piper nodded quickly as more Star Darlings joined them.

Lady Stella, along with Lady Cordial, was already waiting on the deck. She beckoned Piper closer. "The Star Wranglers are still monitoring the skies," she explained. She smiled warmly at Piper. "You'll be on the first star they—"

"Catch," finished Piper.

Lady Stella gave her a funny look. "Is everything okay, Piper? It seems—"

"I've been interrupting a lot lately." Piper nodded.

"Everything's fine," said Piper. She smiled at the head-mistress. "Any last-minute advice?"

Piper managed to hold her tongue while Lady Stella ticked off some items: "Keep checking energy levels on your Wish Pendant. While you should be aware of time passing, don't rush through wish iden-tification. Use your emotions. And be careful not to lose anything."

With that, Lady Cordial passed Piper her special backpack and dangling keychain. "Y-y-y-y-yes," she added. "Keep these items close by at all t-t-t-times."

That reminded Piper: she wanted to place some spe-cial things of her own in the backpack: two sleep masks and her serenity stone. Who knew what would happen to them when her outfit changed in space?

She reached into one dress pocket and removed the sleep masks. But the other pocket was empty. She'd forgotten the stone. In her mind, she could see it, still resting on a pillow in her room. *Starf!*

By then a wrangler had caught a star and was hold-ing it steady, waiting. Vega hurried over to take both of Piper's hands and say, "You'll be good, you'll be great. You'll tell me about it later; can't wait."

Clover hugged her tightly, then hugged Lady Cordial,

standing next to her. "Well," said Lady Cordial, backing away slightly, "that was s-s-s-sweet."

Everyone else said good-bye quickly, and before Piper knew it, she was rushing through space, starlight flashing, colors flying.

The ride was not smooth. In fact, it was much rougher than Piper had expected. She tried not to worry. But it was frightening to think she was out there in the universe, traveling alone.

"Stop that, Piper!" she told herself. "No negative emotions." Of course, there was always her Mirror Mantra. Even without a mirror, it could provide reassurance. But Piper needed a different phrase, one rooted in the here and now.

Even bumpy journeys could end with smooth landings, she knew. "Bumpy journey, smooth landing. Bumpy journey, smooth landing," she repeated to herself again and again until she believed it.

Piper kept saying the phrase even as she accessed her Wishworld Outfit Selector. But soon she had to stop to recite, "Star light, star bright, the first star I see tonight: I wish I may, I wish I might, have the wish I wish tonight," to transform her skin and hair to Wishworld plain.

Then, just as her Star-Zap flashed PREPARE FOR

LANDING, she saw Wishworld hurtling closer. She closed her eyes tight. "Bumpy journey, smooth landing."

And her feet touched the ground with barely a bounce.

Piper opened her eyes. She was facing a brown wall made, it seemed, out of logs. She turned to her right. There was another wall of logs. She turned to her left and saw another wall and still another. Clearly, she was in some sort of room—an empty room, with no ceiling. Clouds and sky were visible overhead. Piper's heart thudded at the strangeness of it all. Then she heard voices.

"Okay, we're just about set to put the roof on."

"This is going to be one amazing playhouse."

Then there was a much younger voice: "Did you see that bright light, Mommy?"

Suddenly, Piper heard *vrooom* sounds and chains clanking. A pointy roof came down atop the walls, leaving the room in darkness.

Piper's heart beat even faster. Without her serenity stone, Piper rubbed her Wish Pendant bracelets, hoping the smooth jewels would help keep her calm.

With nowhere else to look, Piper gazed at the walls. Then, amazingly, she was gazing *through* the walls! She could see outside! She had sunray vision! That must be her special talent, the ability to see through walls, logs, and who knew what else! She'd discovered it so quickly, without even trying. Surely that was a sign of good things to come.

Piper saw a group of Wishlings, young and old, smiling delightedly outside the walls.

"This is just what this playground needs!" said one female Wishling, holding the hand of a toddler. "Won't this be fun, Sophie?"

A playhouse for little Wishlings! Nothing to be scared of at all. But still, Piper needed to get out. She folded up her star and placed it in the backpack's front pocket just as the door opened and light streamed into the room.

A man stood across from Piper, staring at her in surprise.

"Why, there's a girl in here!" he exclaimed.

"Hello!" Piper said pleasantly. "I was actually just leaving." Before anyone could say anything else, she slipped outside, past the Wishlings' astonished faces, and briskly walked away.

The play space was big and busy, and Piper soon blended in. She paused at the edge to get her bearings.

On a long ramp-like structure, a small Wishling

whooshed down. "Not headfirst!" shrieked a female Wishling—the mom, Piper guessed. Meanwhile, a girl rode past on a very small two-wheeled vehicle, pushing on pedals that moved in circles. "Chloe!" the dad called out. "Where is your helmet?"

Wishlings are very focused on small Wishlings' heads, Piper noted.

She retreated behind a tree and felt her spirits soar. What a great place to land! She'd learned about those areas. What had those Wishlings called it? A playground? She could have sworn Professor Illumia Wickes had called them play-arounds during one of her Star Darlings guest lectures. But really, what difference did it make? She was there, with lots of adorable Wishlings who came up to her waist. They were all too young to be her Wisher, though. Just to make sure, she glanced at her Wish Pendant. The bracelets were still dark. But maybe there'd be older Wishlings nearby, and she wouldn't have far to go.

Piper checked her Star-Zap for directions. It showed the exact route, and it seemed to lead quite far away. Piper sighed. She enjoyed exercise as much as the next Starling—as long as it involved stretching—but right then her Wishling sandal straps were digging into her feet. Made from Wishling material, the sandals didn't mold to her feet like comfy Starling ones. Her long, swirly skirt was nice, though. And her cropped T-shirt, a vibrant emerald color with a rainbow by her heart, was cute and perfect.

The sun was perfect, too, shining brightly with just the right degree of warmth. And Piper felt a tingle all around her, an air of expectancy.

She heard one Wishling mom say to a dad, "I'm so happy spring is finally here!"

The male nodded. "We'll be spending a lot more time here now that the weather is nice." He glanced at the Wishling equivalent of a Star-Zap. *A cell phone*, Piper thought. "Oops. Almost three o'clock. Time for pickup."

Piper watched as the play-around emptied out.

It was the end of the school year, Piper realized, putting together the adults' comments and her tingly feeling. That mix of sadness and excitement, with one staryear ending and a long, lazy vacation ahead. The feeling was the same no matter where someone lived.

Piper moved on, following the coordinates of her Star-Zap. She edged toward the far corner of the play-around, where she saw a gate. She pushed against it. Nothing happened. The gate was locked in some way, and she couldn't find a scanner, of course.

"Excuse me," said a little girl who couldn't have been

more than three Wishworld years old. She lifted a hook-like handle and the gate swung open easily.

"Well!" said Piper. "Star sal—I mean, thank you!" She hoped she wouldn't get locked in somewhere else. There might not be a little Wishling around to help.

Piper continued down a treelined street with small cozy-looking houses. Each one had a wide porch that wrapped around to the back. In front of one, Piper stooped to pick up something from the sidewalk. It was shaped like a tube, about the length of her arm, and wrapped in a clear sleeve. She could read words through the wrapper, although it clearly wasn't a book: *Greenfield Crier*. Greenfield was most likely the town's name, Piper thought. And it was fitting. The town had wide yards and grassy plots along the walkways. But what did *Crier* mean?

Piper pinched the tube to see if it would actually cry. It stayed silent. Then she noticed a man walking up to another house and picking up a tube.

"Late delivery today," he said to Piper, taking off the wrapper and unfurling the tube into flat paper. "I missed it before I left for work. Still, it's nice to look over the newspaper in the afternoon, too!"

A newspaper! She'd learned about that in her Wishers 101 class last year and Professor Elara Ursa had gotten it exactly right. It was exciting to actually hold a newspaper in her very own hands. The professor had said that more and more news was being delivered electronically—like it was on Starland—but many Wishlings still had papers delivered to their homes.

"Are you visiting the Trunks?" the man asked, interrupting her thoughts.

"Trunks?" she repeated. Was he asking if she was visiting trees? "Yes, the Trunks," he repeated, pointing to the house behind her.

"Ah!" Piper said, remembering that Wishlings might be referred to by their last names. The house, and the newspaper, must belong to a family called the Trunks.

"No. I'm just picking up the newspaper for them. There!" She placed it carefully on the front steps and kept walking.

Soon small stores replaced the small homes. Piper walked past a brick building with signs that read GREENFIELD STATION, TICKETS, and TRAIN PLATFORM, THIS WAY. Beside the platform, Piper saw what looked like a ladder running on the ground, with yet another sign: BE CAREFUL ON TRACKS.

Two identical little buildings with windows all in a row and wheels at the bottom were parked on the side. *Greenfield Local* was painted on one, *Greenfield Express* on the other. *Can these houses actually move?* Piper wondered. It seemed doubtful.

Piper kept walking, and the sidewalk grew more crowded. Some Wishlings hurried into and out of stores, carrying sacks. Others walked more slowly while chatting with friends. She passed the Coffee Corner. Peeking inside, she saw everyone drinking out of mugs and cups. Coffee, she remembered reading in a holo-textbook, was a staple of the adult Wishling diet. But she had never realized it was a drink!

Then she stopped in front of a place called the Big Dipper. Her heart skipped at the words. *Home*, she thought. The older Starlings' dorm. It gave her a pang just thinking of Starling Academy while she was here, in a place where she couldn't even leave a children's playaround without help. But what was this place? A line snaked out the door, so it must be popular. People were leaving, gripping cone-shaped holders with scoops of brightly colored food inside.

"Yummy ice cream!" said a Wishling boy walking outside with his mom. *Ice cream!* She'd heard about the frosty dessert, too. Maybe it was called the Big Dipper after an ice cream scooper, not the constellation.

Next Piper passed the Greenfield Library and a

flower shop. Finally, the Star-Zap led Piper to a place called Big Rosie's Diner. It was marked with a glowing star on her Star-Zap screen. She was there. The spot where she would meet her Wisher.

The diner looked a little like one of those vehicles she'd walked by earlier. Only, this one appeared to be stuck in the ground. Pretty flower boxes hung just below its windows. The diner was sweet-looking and inviting, with bells above the door. They jingled when customers came in or went out.

A diner, mused Piper. *That sounds like dinner. It must be some sort of restaurant.* Casually, she strolled closer. A few Wishlings stepped outside. One held the door open, assuming Piper wanted to go inside. She decided she might as well. Her Wisher might already be there.

Nodding her thanks, Piper walked in and smiled. Yes, it was a restaurant! Tables with red-checked tablecloths stood in the center, while booths with red cushions lined the walls. There was a long counter directly in front of her, with lots of activity behind it. Wishling workers— not Bot-Bots!—bustled here and there, busily doing things Piper could only guess at. One sprayed some kind of liquid into glasses from a long hose. Another yelled into a window in the wall, where Wishlings appeared to be cooking in a separate room. "Two number fours, one with everything, one with everything hold the mustard," a cook cried, plopping plates on the window's shelf.

Odd, thought Piper. None of her friends had mentioned that Wishlings used numbers, not names, for food.

Then she noticed a separate counter—more of a desk, really—with a woman seated behind some kind of metal machine.

The woman had short curly hair and a nice smile. She reached for a long flat book and stood up. Obviously, she was going to the library down the street.

Instead of leaving, though, the woman carried the book over to Piper and asked, "Seat at the counter?"

"Yes," Piper agreed. "There are seats at the counter." To demonstrate, she moved closer to a stool and tried to pick it up. It didn't budge. But it did spin around.

"Oh!" said Piper. She couldn't resist sitting on it, pushing off from the counter as it twirled squeakily. "Starmendous!" she said. It reminded her of the starry-go-round rides back home. Of course, those rides flew through the air, too.

The woman held up the book. "Would you like to look at—"

"Your book?" Piper said.

"A menu," the woman answered. She handed it to Piper, who saw it was a list of food choices. "Or are you waiting for—"

"A bus?" finished Piper.

"No," said the woman, looking puzzled. "Friends."

Piper gulped. Her first decision. "Oh, I am waiting," she tried to explain, "but not for friends. Not really. But maybe I will find a friend here. Why else am I here, unless it's to make some sort of connection with a . . ." Her voice trailed off.

She was babbling, she knew, and while the woman waited patiently for Piper to stop talking, she was also giving her a slightly funny look.

"I'll just go outside," Piper finished. Her Wish Pendant was dark, so there really was no reason to stay inside, anyway.

"You do that, honey. There's a nice comfy bench right under the oak tree."

Piper headed outside for the big leafy tree and the bench. A shiny silver plaque was nailed onto the back slats. Piper read the inscription out loud: " 'In memory of Rose MacDonald. Thanks for the great food and the even better company.' "

"In memory of" must mean Rose had completed her Cycle of Life. Big Rosie's must have been her diner. Piper gazed up at the clouds, wondering if Rose's star beamed its light right at that spot. Was the star twinkling right then, unseen, in approval of this mission? Piper's mind was wandering, considering the cosmos and its connection to all life-forms, when a boy and girl walked past.

Piper snapped to attention. Could one of those Wishlings be her Wisher? They both had light hair and similar-shaped noses and lopsided grins. Brother and sister, Piper thought. The two laughed and pushed each other playfully. It was the kind of relationship she'd always wanted with her own brother. She glanced hopefully at her pendant. Nope, it wasn't either of them.

Another girl hurried past, her nose in a book. The pendant stayed dark.

Wishling after Wishling walked by while Piper sat on the bench. Still, there was no sign of her Wisher. "Patience, Piper," she counseled herself. This was such a different, new, and exciting experience. She couldn't quite hold on to her calm. So much could go wrong; so much depended on her.

But she'd been waiting on that bench for a long time. What if there was a problem with her pendant and that was why it wasn't lighting up? She shook the bracelets lightly, then harder and harder.

Stop it, Piper! she ordered. It was time for her Mirror Mantra. She crisscrossed her legs in her favorite meditation pose. "Dreams can come true," she said out loud. "It's your time to shine!" The pane revealed Piper's shimmery skin and hair, but just for an instant, and just for her to see. Immediately, she felt energized.

A moment later, Piper felt a tingle at her wrist. *Finally!* she thought, glancing at her pendant. The bracelets were glowing faintly. Smiling, Piper peered down the street. A group of girls was approaching, and with each step they took, the pendant lit up brighter and brighter.

The girls stopped directly in front of Piper. Her pendant flashed even stronger; the jewels sparkled fiercely. One of these Wishlings was definitely her Wisher.

There were four girls, huddled together so closely Piper couldn't see their faces or hear their words. It didn't seem like happy chatter to Piper, though, with the girls talking about the cute boy in class or the latest fashion. Something was up.

The group broke apart, and three of the girls drew away, leaving one girl standing alone. "Bye, Olivia," the shortest one of the three called back in a commanding way. "Everything will be fine." She tugged at the other two, and they walked quickly away.

Maybe the short girl was the Wisher. Piper thought it was a definite possibility. But she wasn't thrilled. The girl seemed a little bossy.

Meanwhile, the girl left behind—Olivia—stood still for a long moment, lost in thought. Piper gazed at her. She was sweet-looking, with a round face and long dark brown hair pulled into a high ponytail. Her blue eyes were large and searching. Surely, Olivia was a deep thinker. But her eyes had dark circles beneath them, as if she was losing sleep. Piper liked her immediately.

By then the other girls were down the block. Olivia stepped past Piper, heading into the diner, and the pendant glowed with extra intensity.

Piper straightened her shoulders. She had found her Wisher.

CHAPTER
6

Now what? Piper wondered. Should she follow the Wisher and go inside the diner, too? She felt hesitant. The woman at the desk already thought she was strange. And while Piper never minded when other Starlings thought she was a little weird—let's face it, not everyone liked to do downward-facing glion poses while meditating in P.E. class—this seemed different.

Piper cared what these Wishlings thought, and she wanted to make a good impression. Maybe because they were the first Wishlings she'd ever met. And maybe, just maybe, it might help her complete her mission.

Through the glass door, Piper saw Olivia drop her backpack behind the front desk. She gave the curly-haired woman a kiss on the cheek. Then she walked around the long counter and slipped behind it to the other side. She waved hello to a woman wiping up a spill at the other end—a "waitress," Piper had learned—and tied on an apron. It seemed that people, not Bot-Bots, served food on Wishworld.

Olivia works at the diner! Piper realized. Now she had no choice but to go in again. This time, she would think carefully before she spoke.

"Hello," Piper said cautiously to the woman at the desk. Now she saw the woman wore a name tag. "Alice," Piper added.

"Hello again," said Alice. "Have you figured out if you want to—"

"Eat?" said Piper.

"Stay," said Alice.

"Yes, I do." Piper leaned over, closer to Alice. She didn't say anything; she just concentrated on connecting.

A funny expression crossed Alice's face. It was a wistful look, like she was remembering something from long ago. She sniffed deeply. "Rhubarb pie. Strawberry-rhubarb pie with crumb topping." She smiled at Piper. "It smells just like the pie my mom, Rosie, used to make. I didn't even know we were serving it today! Or that anyone else could make it the same way!"

Rosie . . . the plaque on the bench . . . the diner name . . . Piper wanted to ask her more, but she had to focus on the task at hand. Adult Wishlings always smelled favorite desserts from childhood when they got close to Starlings. And those memories made them open to suggestion—and to believing whatever the Starlings told them.

Piper stared into Alice's eyes. "I am Piper, and I am here to help out."

Alice nodded solemnly. Then she called, "Everyone! This is Piper, and she is here to help out."

The cook came from the kitchen, wiping his hands on a dishcloth. "I think I'll whip up a coconut cake. For some reason, there's a smell around here that reminds me of coming home from school and finding a thick slice of cake waiting for me on the kitchen table." He stuck out his hand for Piper to shake. She touched his fingers, unsure what to do. "I'm Pete," he said. "Now, what is your name again?"

"I am Piper," she repeated. "And I am here to help."

"Of course you are," Pete said, slightly dazed. Then he smiled. "We can always use an extra pair of hands around here." He turned to the counter. "Olivia! Come meet our new employee." He stopped, looking confused. "Wait a minute. Not an employee. A helper, I guess."

Olivia walked over. "Just a helper?" she asked Piper. "Why would you want to help without getting a—"

"Star payment," finished Piper. *Oh, Starf!* she thought. That can't be right.

"Um . . . a paycheck," said Olivia.

"It's for a school assignment," Piper told Olivia as the two girls moved off to the side to talk.

"You don't go to the Lincoln School, do you? Where do you go?" Olivia sounded curious, not accusing. But Piper felt angry—at herself: why hadn't she thought about that earlier? Walking over, she had come up with a pretend last name: Smith. She had read somewhere it was a common Wishling name. She had even thought of a pretend address: 123 Main Street, again very common. But her school? She had no idea. And she couldn't very well whip out her Star-Zap to request information about common Wishling school names. Not that it would work anyway!

Her gaze lit on a passing truck that said MAIL DELIVERY.

"Uh, the Mail School?"

"Male School?" Olivia said, puzzled. "You go to a school for boys?"

"No!" Piper said quickly. "It's Mayle . . . M-a-y-l-e, for the name of my town . . . Maylefield!" The name sounded kind of lame, Piper knew. Too much like

Greenfield. But it was the best she could do with hardly any time to think.

"Maylefield," mused Olivia. She shook her head. "I've never heard of it."

Piper smiled. She had this part covered. "Oh, it's floozels . . . I mean miles . . . away. And we're on vacation this week so I'm visiting my grandmother. I'm doing a work-study program for extra credit," she said.

Olivia nodded. "Extra credit is good," she said thoughtfully. "It could bring up your grade so you don't get anxious when you take a test. It's kind of like being thrown one of those rescue rings lifeguards use to save people from drowning."

Piper had just studied beach recreation in Wishling Ways, and she could picture the safety device—like a floating doughnut. Then, just as Olivia started talking again, she had another vision. It was from a bad dream. She was trying to swim to shore at Luminous Lake, but that same evil presence she'd felt before was trying to pull her down . . . down.

"So if you have that sinking feeling during a test, you—" Olivia was saying with a laugh.

"Go underwater," Piper finished for her. "You don't scream, you don't breathe, you don't even think."

Olivia took a step back, startled by the dark image.

"No . . . I was going to say that you can just relax. It would make you feel better knowing you had help—like a rescue ring."

Relaxation! Piper, of all Starlings on Starland, knew about relaxation. Why hadn't she gotten that right away? And now she'd scared poor Olivia on top of everything else. Not the best way to connect!

"So did Olivia tell you that anyone who works here is part of our family? Just like Big Rosie used to say?" Alice came over to put an arm around Piper.

"No, I didn't," Olivia said, taking another step away from Piper.

"Well, we're one big family here," Alice went on. "Pete is my husband, and Olivia is our daughter. Rosie was my mom, Olivia's grandmother. She started the diner."

"Wow," said Piper. "That's so nice that you're all together. And it's nice that you're keeping the diner in the family."

Olivia smiled but stayed where she was. "It is nice!" she agreed. "Big Rosie started a great tradition. But she wasn't really very big," Olivia confided, clearly happy to have someone to talk to about her grandmother. "She was actually shorter than you, Piper—and even shorter than my friend Morgan. And she was really skinny, especially for someone who spent so much time in kitchens! But she had a big, big personality!" She paused. "I really—"

"Miss her," Piper finished. "I'm sure you do," she added quietly as Alice went to help a customer. "My granddad left us, too, and it's sad. But I think of him so often and imagine conversations. So sometimes I really feel like he's here with me. Star apologies for your loss."

Piper ended her speech with such warmth and understanding that Olivia's eyes filled. Later, Piper realized she'd used the Starland saying. Luckily, Olivia was more focused on the meaning than the actual words.

Piper sighed. Olivia's family was making her think of her own. Her brother, Finn, never very talkative, could still be a comfort. They were related, after all, and she never had to explain little things to him, let alone big things.

"Do you have brothers or sisters?" she asked Olivia.

Olivia brightened. "Yes, a sister. And she's coming home from college for the summer in May."

A grown-up Wishling, coming up to the counter, overheard. "Oh, your sister Isabel!" she said. "My son was in class with her all through elementary school, middle school, and high school. She was always an amazing student. Straight As in every class. I heard she never got a grade below that, in fact!" She turned to Alice, a hint of jealousy in her eyes. "You must be very proud."

"Yes, we are," said Alice. Piper was watching Olivia. While the woman was speaking, she had seemed to freeze, barely moving a muscle. But when Alice reached over to squeeze her arm and say, "And we're just as proud of Olivia," she grinned, and Piper thought maybe she had imagined it.

Anyway, it was time to get to know Olivia—to see her in action and figure out her wish. "Do you want to show me around so I can start helping?" she asked.

"Of course," Olivia said happily. "We're not some big fancy restaurant. My mom likes to run everything the old-fashioned way, just like Grandma Rosie did. Anyway, there's the cash register." She pointed to the machine on Alice's desk, and Piper nodded like she understood what it meant.

Next Olivia led Piper behind the counter and showed her different workstations. The front station directly behind the counter held ice cream freezers, coffee machines, and a small refrigerator to store juice and milk.

Ice cream! Coffee! Piper knew the words. She'd even seen ice cream and coffee for herself. But she still needed

to study them—and everything else!—to truly understand. Piper took out her Star-Zap, hoping Olivia would
think it was just a regular cell phone. She pretended to
hold it casually, the way she'd seen Wishlings do, when
really she was taking holo-vids and recording Olivia's
voice.

Olivia gestured for Piper to follow her into the
kitchen, then stopped by another workstation. "This
area is for roll-ups," Olivia explained.

Hmmm, roll-ups. Piper knew about push-ups and pull-
ups from Physical Energy class. Perhaps roll-ups were
another form of exercise. But truth be told, she'd never
paid much attention. She'd discovered a starmat hidden
behind some equipment in the gym, and if she wandered
slowly to that corner, no one noticed. So while everyone
else jumped and ran, she just meditated quietly. She was
pretty sure Coach Geeta knew what she was up to but
never called her on it. Most likely, the coach understood
that Piper got more energy from meditating than from
playing star ball.

"So," Piper said to Olivia, "you keep in shape while
you're working by rolling up?"

"No!" Olivia giggled. She grabbed a napkin. And
before Piper could even blink, she had rolled a knife,

fork, and spoon inside the napkin in such a way that it stayed wrapped even when she flipped it in the air. It was almost like magic.

"This is part of side work, and for now you should just focus on this kind of stuff. Roll-ups, refilling ketchup"—she pointed to squeezable containers that came to a point, filled with an unappetizing red liquid mixture—"and sugar dispensers. No waiting on tables. Not yet, anyway."

"Okay." Piper kept nodding as if she understood. Hopefully, it would all make sense when she studied everything later. It turned out, though, there wasn't time.

"You can start right now and refill the sugar dispensers," Olivia said. She took out a tray of empty dispensers. Then she waved toward a high shelf where a dozen large containers stood in a line.

Piper opened her mouth, about to explain how clueless she was, when the phone in front rang. Olivia backed away to answer it. "Okay, you're on your own," she told Piper.

Piper paced in front of the containers. Which one held the sugar? She glanced around helplessly and looked straight through the cabinet door above the containers. There were unopened jars labeled MUSTARD and PICKLES, plus bags labeled SALT, PEPPER, and—Piper grinned—SUGAR!

She took out the bag, then used her sunray vision to see what sugar actually looked like. Okay, now she realized the sugar dispenser was the third from the right. When she lifted the container off the shelf, though, she had to laugh. It was labeled on the lid!

Now Piper had the dispenser. She had the sugar. She'd even found a scooper. She mentally patted herself on the back for that one.

It should be simple from here on, she thought. The dispenser had a hole on top, and the sugar should slide right in.

She ladled out a heaping scoop from the container and poured the sugar over the dispenser. Sugar granules bounced off the top with a *ping ping ping* and scattered all over the floor. Only a few granules actually made it into the dispenser. Piper tried again and again with the same results.

"This is going to take a starday and a half," she told herself. But she had to do it. She would acknowledge these negative feelings so they would pass like drifting clouds; then she'd get back to work.

She reached once again for the scooper. But then

Pete walked in, holding another sugar dispenser—this one with its top screwed off. "Here's one more for you," he said.

After that, it was easy to fill the dispensers. She just took off each lid, poured in the sugar, then closed it up. A short time later, she was done. But the table and floor were still covered with sugar. Piper gazed down, dismayed. Why couldn't the floor be self-cleaning?

"That's okay, honey," Alice said, coming over to inspect the mess. "But it always makes me me feel better to leave a workstation as clean—"

"As you found it," Piper finished.

"You too?" said Alice. "Good. Just use the broom and dustpan in the corner."

Another confusing task! Piper eyed the long stick with bristles on one end in the corner. It didn't look like any kind of pan, so that must be the broom. Experimenting, she pushed it along the floor. To her surprise, it moved the sugar granules into a neat pile, almost by itself! Then she swept it all into the flat pan-thing that had been next to it.

She gazed at the pan a moment, half expecting the sugar to disappear into thin air. But of course, she was on Wishworld, not Starland, and the pan stayed full. *Next step: find a garbage can.* She spied one in the opposite corner and hurried over. *Ewww!* She wrinkled her nose. It was stuffed with actual garbage that smelled. No vanishing garbage cans here! *Disgusting!* Quickly, she dumped the sugar on top, then turned on her heel.

"Nice work," said Alice, returning. "Olivia is in a booth in the back, doing homework. Why don't you join her, and in a little while you two can have dinner here? The least we can do is feed you!"

Olivia grinned. Her first Wishling compliment—it felt almost like Star Kindness Day. Now to find Olivia. She walked around the diner tables, all the way to the back and the very last booth.

Schoolbooks were spread across the table, along with pencils and pens and notebooks. But there was no sign of Olivia.

Piper's heart sank. She'd spent way too much time filling sugar dispensers. And now look what had happened. She'd lost her Wisher!

CHAPTER
7

Piper had no idea what to do next. So she sat down in the booth and idly leafed through the books, thinking. Wishling books were so heavy and cumbersome. How did students carry them around, much less hold them up to read?

"Concentrate, Piper," she told herself. "Focus on Olivia!"

Where could she be? Why had she left so suddenly? Would she return?

Piper pushed aside *Our Nation's History Through the Centuries* to clear space to put her head down. She always thought better that way. But the history textbook bumped the math book, which nudged something called

Advanced Reading Material for the Young Scholar, and they all fell onto the seat across the table.

"Ouch!" Olivia popped up, rubbing her shoulder. The books thudded to the floor.

"You were resting here the whole time?" Piper was amazed. "I'm so sorry I interrupted your time of rejuvenation."

"Huh?" Olivia sounded confused. She blinked and shook her head. "I must have fallen asleep."

Piper nodded encouragingly. It certainly made sense to sleep in the late afternoon. Although, as a general rule, she preferred an earlier naptime.

Olivia yawned. "I've been so tired lately."

Piper leaned closer, a tingle of excitement running down her spine. Clearly, Olivia wasn't getting enough sleep. Most likely, she was anxious about a problem; worrying could keep anyone awake. And her wish must revolve around solving the problem.

But what was the problem?

Piper could almost feel the wish dangling in front of her, tantalizingly, as if she could reach out and touch it.

"Sometimes I have trouble sleeping, too," Piper told Olivia in a way meant to encourage her to tell more. That was stretching the truth. So Piper crossed her legs at the ankles the way Starlings did if they told a fib.

"You do?" Olivia took a deep breath. "Usually I fall asleep as soon as my head hits the pillow and I don't wake up until my alarm goes off. But lately I've been—"

"Sensing an evil presence lurking in your dreams. Dark and threatening. You can almost see it in your mind's eye whenever you close your eyes. . . ."

Piper's voice trailed off when she caught sight of Olivia's put-off expression. "Uh, no," Olivia said, leaning back against the bench, farther away from Piper.

"Oh, *starf*," Piper muttered to herself. Now she had really freaked out her Wisher. And she really needed to gain Olivia's trust. It was so important in pinpointing the correct wish.

"Don't mind me," she said airily, as if didn't matter that much. "That whole 'evil presence' stuff? It was just part of a bad dream I had the other night."

Olivia smiled sadly. "I've been having bad dreams, too," she confided. But then she seemed to pull back once more and shrugged. "It's really no big deal. Everyone has bad dreams. I'm sure they'll just go away."

She didn't sound like she believed it. And Piper didn't believe it, either. Bad dreams had a way of sticking around until you figured out what they meant.

"Girls!" Alice called from behind the counter. "Come and get your dinner."

Reluctantly, Piper stood when Olivia did. They made their way to the front of the diner, where two heaping plates of food were waiting. Piper stared at her dish. She didn't recognize a thing. So she grabbed a nearby menu and leafed through the pages. There were tons of choices. How could she figure out what she was eating?

Her eyes stopped at the entry HOT DOG. She gasped. Wasn't that a Wishling pet? But right next to the words was a picture of a cylinder-shaped food in a bun. It looked nothing at all like those cute four-legged creatures. Luckily, there were other pictures, too. Piper identified her food as a veggie burger, sweet potato fries, one of those long green and bumpy things called a pickle, and coleslaw. She couldn't guess what that was, even squinting at the photo.

Partial to greens, she started with the pickle. It reminded her of cukumbrella, a crunchy vegetable that didn't need much light to grow. There were always lots to be found in the Flats.

Piper picked up her knife and fork to cut the pickle. But Olivia was just holding hers in one hand, so Piper did the same. *When on Wishworld, do as Wishlings do,* she thought. That was one of the sayings professors were always spouting. She took a big bite. Sour! Everything else was delicious, though. Piper decided she'd have this for every meal on Wishworld if she could.

In record time, Piper finished her dinner. Traveling to Wishworld used up so much energy! She had definitely needed to replenish. Meanwhile, Olivia just pushed her food around the plate. Piper was sure she was still thinking about her bad dream. If only she could get Olivia to open up again. She had to try. And this time, she'd take it slow.

"Maybe you'd like something else to eat?" she asked gently. "Some kind of comfort food?" Eating garble greens always made Piper feel better. "I can get it for you."

"Good idea, Piper. Comfort food! But I'll take care of it myself." Olivia jumped off her stool, went around the counter, and started working by the fountain area.

Piper grinned.

Olivia smiled back as she grabbed two tall glasses. In each, she put a spoonful of chocolate syrup and some milk. Then she filled the glasses with cold seltzer from the fountain tap. Olivia named everything as she went, so it was easy to follow.

Piper could barely contain her excitement when she heard *chocolate*. Even though she'd eaten a big dinner, she still had to try the tasty treat she'd heard about from other Star Darlings. But she did have to ask about the seltzer.

"Oh, it's just bubbly water," Olivia explained, adding a bit more.

The drinks foamed to the brim, without one drop spilling over. Olivia mixed the glasses with a long spoon and plopped in straws. Then she pushed one across to Piper.

"Try it!" she said.

Piper sipped. "Startast—I mean fantastic!" The drink was starmazingly refreshing, with a yummy chocolate sweetness to it. But it had a fizz and pop, too, and might just have been the best thing Piper had ever tasted. Other Star Darlings had talked about soda and chocolate milk, but she doubted anyone else had had one of these on her mission. "What is it called?"

"It's a chocolate egg cream. I know, I know," Olivia added quickly. "It doesn't have eggs or cream. So don't ask me why it's called an egg cream. And I'm not surprised you don't know it. Hardly anyone outside of New York City has heard about it."

New York City? The place name meant nothing to Piper. She supposed it was a very small town in the middle of nowhere. It had to be, for hardly anyone to know about this wonderful drink.

Piper reached for her trusty menu to find the listing. "Oh, you won't find it there," Olivia said. "People wouldn't order it, anyway. It's just a New York thing. You know my parents are from there."

"Okay, girls," said Alice, reaching to clear Piper's empty glass. "It's getting late. Time for you to head out." She looked at Piper. "Is someone coming to pick you up?"

Piper concentrated. Staring into Alice's eyes, she said solemnly, "Why don't I sleep over at your house?"

Alice sniffed the air. "There's that rhubarb pie smell again. How strange. Pete isn't even baking today!" Then she looked at Piper. "Why don't you sleep over at our house?"

Olivia looked surprised but not upset. A favorable sign, Piper thought.

"Sounds good," said Piper. "I'm sure my grandma won't mind." Holding in her laughter, she pretended to place a call on her Star-Zap. Her family had no idea she was on Wishworld. But she felt sure that if they had, they'd have been fine with her spending the night with this nice family.

The two girls cleared the rest of their dishes, then made their way to Olivia's home. It was just around the corner from the diner, on a street very much like the one she'd walked down earlier, with snug little houses and big leafy trees.

To open the front door, Olivia used a metal tool, twisting it into a hole below a knob. The inside of the house was just like the outside, Piper thought: cozy and colorful, with shaggy rugs covering brightly polished hardwood floors, small rooms, and lots of knickknacks spread on shelves and cabinet tops. In one alcove, framed photos and awards covered the wall. Piper examined them all closely.

In most pictures, Olivia posed with an older girl who had the same deep blue eyes. "Is this your sister?" Piper asked.

"Yup," said Olivia. "Isabel."

Isabel's awards took up more space than Olivia's, Piper noticed. But that was probably because she was older. She'd finished more school years. "You both are excellent students," Piper observed.

Piper meant it as a compliment. She expected Olivia to say thank you or at least acknowledge the comment in some way. But Olivia leaned over her backpack as if she didn't want to continue the conversation. She pulled out some textbooks and said, "I'll do my homework now if you don't—"

"Mind," Piper finished for her. "Why would I mind? You feel like I'm a real guest, I know, and like you're responsible for me. But I basically invited myself. Do your homework."

Olivia finished her homework at the dining room table while Piper browsed through her schoolbooks. She couldn't get over the feel of them. They were heavy, true, but wonderful, too. The textbook pages were so smooth and shiny and fun to turn. After about an hour, Alice came home from the diner and announced, "Bedtime!"

Olivia pushed aside dozens of stuffed animals on her bedroom floor and set up a blow-up bed for Piper. She opened a drawer to show Piper pair after pair of pajamas. Piper lifted a gauzy scoop-necked nightgown, the color of Luminous Lake. "Could I wear this one?" she asked.

"Of course," said Olivia. Without even looking, she took the first pair of pajamas from the pile and went to the bathroom to change. It always amazed Piper that most Starlings paid so little attention to their nightwear. She guessed Wishlings did the same.

The girls settled into their beds quietly. *That has to change; we need to connect,* Piper thought. And really, it was the perfect time. There was something about talking in the dark, right before you fell asleep, that was tailor-made for confidences.

"So," Piper said, pulling the blanket up to her chin, "tell me about a typical day here in Greenfield. Then I'll tell you about my days in Ladyfield."

"Ladyfield?" Olivia repeated. "I thought you were from Maylefield!"

Piper groaned to herself. Why couldn't she keep these things straight? Sometimes she was too dreamy for her own good. "Just testing you," Piper said. "You passed."

"Oh, okay. Well"—Olivia fluffed up her pillow—"about my day. I set my alarm for six-fifteen. It's early. I know. We don't have to be in school until nine, but I have to—"

"Give yourself plenty of time, in case you have more bad dreams and need to shake off that feeling of impending doom."

"Ummm. No. I have to go to the diner to eat breakfast."

Piper considered this. Olivia went to the diner before school and after school. That was a lot of time spent away from home. Could that have something to do with her wish? Most likely, yes. She should definitely look into this more.

"Okay, breakfast. So then what?" Piper prompted her.

"Then my friends meet me in front of the diner and we—"

"Discuss any disturbing dreams you may have had the night before," Piper finished.

"Walk to school together," Olivia said, moving closer to the wall, putting more and more distance between them.

But Piper had to keep trying.

"And then school?"

"School is just plain old school." Now Olivia actually turned her back on Piper. "And then I head back to the diner after."

The diner again! Olivia was there way too often, and it was obviously stressing her out. It sounded like she was working an awful lot. Maybe she wanted to be home instead. Maybe she wanted to join an after-school club or play a sport. Although Piper didn't see the appeal, many Starlings did, and it was really good for them! But once again, Piper was getting off track. *Olivia, Olivia*, she told herself.

"Well, I'm here now," she said to Olivia. "I can cover for you at the diner so you don't have to work so much. Wouldn't that be great?"

"Oh, no! I love working there," Olivia told her, sounding annoyed. "I don't *have* to go. I go because I *want* to." She yawned. "I'm getting kind of tired," she said pointedly.

Uh-oh. All Olivia wanted to do was sleep, but Piper kept asking irritating questions. Suddenly, a thought popped into her head, and she sat up.

"What?" Olivia said, sounding even more annoyed.

"Don't worry," said Piper. "I won't ask you any more questions. I just had an idea. If you like, I could show you some ways to relax. I know some techniques that may help you sleep."

"Really?" said Olivia, interested. She sat up, too.

Piper nodded.

"Okay," Olivia agreed. "Let's do it."

"First, let's both lie back down." It wouldn't hurt Piper to de-stress, too. "Now we close our eyes and focus on breathing. Deep breath in. Deep breath out. Deep breath in. Deep breath out."

Together, the girls breathed, keeping their eyes shut tight.

"Now we're going to focus on each part of our body, to help it relax. Start with the toes on your right foot. Tense those toe muscles for a count of ten. One, two, three . . ." Piper spoke slowly and softly. "Now relax those same muscles for another count of ten."

Of course, Piper couldn't see Olivia with her own eyes closed. But as they worked from the toes to the legs, to the arms and up, she could sense a peace coming over the Wishling. By the end, Piper was as loose as a rag doll. She felt herself drifting off to sleep. *I hope this helps Olivia*, she thought.

Piper was dreaming. She was floating on her back in a warm stream. Her skin tingled in the fresh air, and all was right with the cosmos. She gazed up at the starry sky, listening to the peaceful sound of water lapping against the shore. Suddenly, the calm gurgles turned into frenzied gasps.

It wasn't the sound of the stream. It was someone struggling to breathe.

Piper shot up, wide-awake. Her heart was beating quickly. She could see Olivia in the dim light, shaking and heaving, trying to catch her breath.

"Are you okay?" Piper climbed into bed beside Olivia.

Olivia nodded, her eyes half closed. She held up a finger, the universal sign for *Wait*, and slowly her breathing returned to normal. Piper brushed a strand of hair from Olivia's eyes. Her forehead felt damp and cold with sweat. Piper wished she could make that scared feeling disappear like a puff of stardust.

"I had another nightmare," Olivia finally said.

Piper held her close, murmuring words her mother used to say after she and her brother had bad dreams. "Hush, hush, I'm right here. It's over now. It will be all right."

And it would be all right. Piper just had to identify the correct wish and help Olivia make it come true. Then everything would be fine. And Piper felt sure she was on the right track. Olivia might not be working too hard, but Piper was sure her wish had to do with the diner. She'd barely mentioned anything else!

Still, Piper thought ruefully, she'd felt sure the relaxation exercise would help Olivia get a good night's sleep. And look how that had turned out. It hadn't done a star-blessed thing.

CHAPTER
8

True to her word, Olivia's cell phone alarm went off at 6:15 the next morning. That was way too early for Piper, who liked to sleep as late as possible and still make it to breakfast in time.

Olivia didn't seem particularly happy to get up, either. But she trudged around the room, grabbing clothes.

Meanwhile, Piper stretched lazily on her bed. Maybe she didn't actually have to get up now. True, it was a school day, but only for Olivia. Piper's pretend school was on vacation this week. She really didn't need to spend the day in class. While she was curious about Wishling schools (Did the students really take notes by hand, writing down everything the teachers said, without recording a thing? How quaint!), she was more interested in completing her mission. And Piper felt positive that

Olivia's wish had to do with Big Rosie's.

"I really should spend another day at the diner for my assignment," she told Olivia. "Do you mind if I don't go to school with you?"

Olivia laughed. "I didn't expect you to go with me! Why would you think that? You're on vacation!"

Piper laughed, too. It was because all the other Star Darlings had gone to school so far. "Oh, I was just kidding," she said.

Olivia nodded distractedly as she tried to fit all her books in her backpack. "I've got to hurry now. I'll tell my parents you'll go to the diner when you're ready. You can eat there. Just close the front door of the house on your way out."

Olivia was certainly organized when she needed to be! "Sounds like a plan." Piper yawned and pulled the blanket over her head. Just a few more starmins of rest and she'd be raring to go. She didn't even hear Olivia leave. She was already sound asleep.

ZZZZZ! ZZZZZZ! A loud startling noise, like the biggest swarm of glitterbees imaginable, woke up Piper. She glanced at the clock. *Hmmm.* That was a bit more than a few starmins.

ZZZZZ! ZZZZZZZ!

Moon and stars! What was that sound? If Olivia heard that every morning, no wonder she was having nightmares. Piper rolled off her cot and shuffled to the window.

A grown-up Wishling was riding some sort of machine. Grass and dirt spurted out one side, and the grass seemed to shorten as he rode over it.

Starland's grass always looked immaculate but never actually needed cutting. These poor Wishlings had so many chores it was no wonder they looked harried.

Anyway, it was time to start her starday; her last on Wishworld, Piper felt sure. Now that she'd figured out that Olivia's wish concerned the diner, she just had to get to Big Rosie's to discover the details.

A little while later, Alice met Piper at the diner door, swinging it open and waving her inside. "Piper! I am so glad you're here! Usually we have two waitresses working the morning shift. But Donna called in sick. It would be great if you could take care of customers today." She paused. "Only if you're comfortable waiting tables, of course."

Piper's eyes opened wide. The previous day, all she had done was fill some sugar dispensers, and that hadn't gone well at all. Could she possibly be a waitress? And keep all the orders straight?

Piper breathed deeply. Of course she could. She just had to stay calm and focused. Besides, how could she say no? Big Rosie's Diner needed her help!

"Sure," Piper said gamely. "Where do I start?"

Alice beamed. "Diane will show you the ropes."

Now there were ropes involved. Waiting tables sounded complicated already.

"This is Diane," Alice went on as a woman walked by holding a tray of dirty glasses. Diane paused but didn't smile.

"Don't worry. Diane's just a little grouchy this morning. She'll warm up to you." Alice nudged Piper toward the kitchen. "Go on. Follow her. She'll show you what to do."

In the kitchen, Diane eyed Piper's outfit: loose bright green drawstring pants that swept the floor, a flowery top with long bell sleeves, and delicate-looking sandals. All suitable for lounging, but not really for waitressing. "Do you have anything else to wear?" she asked.

Piper looked at Diane. She wore a knee-length black skirt, a button-down white shirt, and sensible black lace-up shoes.

"Be right back," Piper said. She ducked into the bathroom, accessed her Wishworld Outfit Selector, and emerged wearing ankle-length black pants and a neat white shirt, with just one small flower on the front pocket. Her black shoes looked just like Diane's.

Diane nodded at the outfit then spent the next half hour explaining how to set tables and write up orders on the pad, when to pick up food, and, it seemed to Piper, about a moonium other things.

For once, Piper didn't interrupt. She just listened intently. She was excited to write on paper with a writing utensil.

Diane checked the clock. "It's time for the morning rush," she said, "so get ready." Then she disappeared into the back just as the doorbells jingled. A mom carrying a baby walked in, followed a few starmins later by an elderly man. Alice led them to their tables. But then other customers were coming in, too.

Piper took a deep breath and glanced in the mirror. "Dreams can come true," she said. "It's your time to shine!"

She could do this.

Smiling steadily, Piper walked to the older man. He had silvery hair that circled his head, with a large bald spot right in the center, and a big bushy mustache that matched.

Piper placed a glass of water on the table. Then she flipped open her pad and stood poised, pen in hand, to take his order. "What would you like, sir?" she asked in a pleasant voice.

"What?" he said, clearly surprised. "Don't you know?"

"Ummm . . ." Piper hedged. Was she supposed to read customers' minds, too? She tried, concentrating her energy on his thoughts. And while she picked up that he was feeling impatient and a little put out, she couldn't for the starlife of her figure out what he wanted to eat.

"I have the same thing every morning," the man said. "Haven't you—"

"Waited on you before?" Piper shook her head. "No, I'm new."

"Okay, here's what I get. Three egg whites scrambled, omelet-style, a whole-wheat bagel with the center scooped out, an extra plate to put the bagel on, no home fries, and two low-fat cream cheeses."

Piper wrote furiously to take it all down.

"And a cup of—"

"Zing?" Piper asked.

"No, coffee," he replied. "What in the world is Zing?"

Oops, thought Piper. *There I go again.*

"Let me handle Lou," Diane said on her way to the kitchen. "He can get a little grumpy if you don't get everything exactly right."

"No, no," Piper insisted. The diner was filling up.

Other people were taking seats. And Piper wanted to prove herself. "I want to do this," she told Diane. Then she paused. "Just tell me what a bagel is."

Time passed in a haze. After an hour, Piper found an elastic band and loosely tied back her hair so it wouldn't get in the way. After another hour, she retied it in a high, severe ponytail.

No doubt about it, waitressing was hard work—always hurrying from customer to customer, from kitchen to table. But it wasn't only physical. It took mental energy, too.

At one point, Piper was turning the corner carrying a tray of dirty dishes back to the kitchen. She heard Diane say, "Corner." Piper had no idea what that meant until Diane flew around the corner and the two bumped. They were both carrying loaded trays, and plates crashed to the floor, shattering into little pieces. Now the floor had to be cleaned and Diane's food prepared again.

"Next time I yell 'corner,'" Diane said through gritted teeth, "stop if you're nearby. It means I'm coming around it."

Another time, Pete shouted from the kitchen, "Burgers, eighty-six!" So Piper helpfully, or so she thought, began to carefully count eighty-six plates for the eighty-six burgers. But Pete had only frowned when she brought them over. "That means we're out of burgers," he explained in a tense voice. A little while later, he called out that the lunch special was "on the fly." Piper ducked to avoid the flying chicken potpie. Only later did she learn that *on the fly* meant Pete was cooking something quickly.

Each of those times, Piper had almost lost control. She'd felt tears slip out of her eyes, a burning sensation in her cheeks, and a knot forming in her stomach. But then she had retreated to a quiet spot in the back and visualized herself floating carefree in Luminous Lake. Moments later, she'd been ready for more customers.

By the time lunch was in full swing, Piper didn't feel frazzled at all. She glided around the diner, quickly but smoothly, pausing to take deep breaths every once in a while but managing to stay unruffled. If only the Star Darlings could see her now, she thought—especially practical Vega, who always had everything under control. Dreamy, absentminded Piper was holding down a complicated Wishling job!

Piper considered it a minor victory when Lou came back for lunch and asked for her specifically. Maybe it was because she smiled at him. She smiled at everyone. But not every customer smiled back. In a job like this, she realized, you saw the best and worst of Wishlings.

"Busy day," Diane said to Piper when there was a lull in customer traffic. Diane had definitely warmed up to her. She lowered her voice to add, "And that's unusual lately. You know. . . ." She nodded across the street, to a restaurant with a big yellow-and-black BB on its sign. "'Your local Busy Bee,'" Piper read from the sign, "'the buzz-iest place in town. Five billion served.'"

"Ever since that fast food place opened," Diane continued, "business has been slower than usual."

Piper understood the slow business part. But fast food? She pictured hamburgers and French fries with little legs, racing around a restaurant.

"Lots of customers have started eating across the street." Diane shook her head. "The prices may be cheaper, but you can't compare the quality. This right here"—she tapped the counter—"is real home cooking. Just like—"

"Bot-Bot cooks used to make," Piper finished.

"Huh?" said Diane. "I was going to say 'Mom.' Like my mom used to make."

"Of course," Piper agreed. "That's what I call my mom. Bot-Bot. It's from when I was a baby." Of course, *mom* and *Bot-Bot* sounded nothing at all alike. But it was the best Piper could do. "I have no idea why."

Diane shrugged at the explanation. "Alice and Pete will never admit it. But they're feeling stressed about the business."

Piper's heart thumped at the word *stressed. Aha*, she thought. *If Alice and Pete are stressed about customers, then Olivia must be, too.* That was the problem.

I've identified the wish! she thought. She didn't feel any energy, but she knew not all Starlings did. Well, hopefully she had identified it. Piper knew not to count her stars just yet. Fifty percent of wishes were misidentified, after all.

Still, Olivia's wish seemed clear enough: she wanted the diner to have more customers! If the diner did more business, Olivia would feel better and her bad dreams would end.

"Waitress!" someone called out to Piper, interrupting her thoughts. Piper had seen Diane flinch when a customer called her "waitress," though most knew her by name. Greenfield was a small town, after all. But being called "waitress" made Piper feel proud. She looked out the diner window to see a dad lifting his son out of the backseat of a car. He slammed the door shut and the two walked into the diner. The boy didn't look happy. His face was streaked with dirt, and tears had left clean little trails down to his chin.

Before Piper could say a word, the boy started to wail. "Where Harvey?" he cried. "Where Harvey?"

"I'm sorry," said the man. "Harvey is my son's—"

"Best friend?" Piper suggested.

"No, his bunny," he explained.

"I'm sorry, sir," Piper said to the father. Her heart went out to the little boy, but she was proud to know that a bunny was a Wishworld animal with long floppy ears. "We don't allow pets in the diner."

"No, no," the father said. "Harvey is his stuffed animal." He turned to his son. "It's okay, Sammy. We'll find that lost bunny. I promise. But right now, we're going to order you a special treat."

But Sammy didn't want ice cream, pie, rice pudding, or Jell-O. He just wanted Harvey back. Piper's own mind flashed back to the day before and how a special treat seemed to cheer up Olivia—if only momentarily. "I know just the thing," she said.

She disappeared behind the counter. Then she set to work making two chocolate egg creams. "Chocolate syrup," she told herself, "milk, and seltzer. No eggs. No cream."

"Are you making egg creams?" Alice asked, moving closer. "We don't sell them; they're not even on the menu. Why would a customer even order it?"

Piper flushed, hoping she hadn't made a mistake. "They didn't," she said. "I just made it for them. Is that okay?"

Alice thought a moment. "Yes, I guess it is. It's already made, anyway. So just go ahead and serve it. I'll figure out how much to charge."

"Thanks!" said Piper, relieved she wouldn't have to disappoint the father. His son had settled down a bit and was just sniffling. But anything could set him off again.

A starsec later, she placed two tall glasses on their table. "Here!"

Sammy slurped through his straw while his father watched. "Yummy!" the boy said, grinning ear to ear.

Then the dad sipped his own egg cream and smiled. "It *is* good!" he exclaimed. "What do you call this?"

"It's a chocolate egg cream," Piper told him. "And you can't get it at any fast food restaurant." Piper tapped her elbows three times for luck. At least she hoped you couldn't get it at any fast food restaurant. What about places in that small town called New York City?

"Well, that's for sure," Alice said from across the room, and Piper felt better.

"Sweet," said the dad, who took out his phone and, oddly enough to Piper, took a photo of the egg cream.

"Hey, Alice!" a customer at the counter called out. "Can I get one of those egg dreams?"

"Egg creams," Alice corrected. "And yes!"

"Me too," someone else shouted "They look really good!"

Just then a wail echoed through the diner. "My bunny," Sammy cried again. The egg cream finished, he'd remembered his lost stuffed animal.

All of a sudden, a picture appeared in Piper's mind: a raggedy stuffed bunny on a Wishling car floor. Every once in a while she'd get a hunch or instinct—she didn't know what to call it. But she'd learned to trust it.

She peered through the diner window, into the car they had exited. She looked through the car doors. Like magic, the metal melted away to reveal the floor, covered by books, toys, and a blanket. And underneath the blanket, Piper could see the missing bunny. "Hey," she said, as casually as she could. "Did you check the backseat?"

The dad sighed. "I already looked."

Then he sniffed the air and got a wistful look on his face. "Mmm," he said. "Apple cobbler. Just like my aunt Kitty used to make." He smiled. "I'll go check again right now." He hurried outside with Sammy. Starmins later they were back, Sammy clutching his precious bunny tightly.

"Thank you, thank you," his father said to Piper. "I

don't know how you knew where to look. You're a life-saver." Sammy hugged her, which made Piper glow for a split starsec, too quick for anyone to notice. Then the dad left an extra-big tip.

It had taken a while for Piper to figure out the tip business. First of all, there was no physical money on Starland so the bills and coins themselves were odd to her. And it seemed strange that Wishlings would just leave money lying on tables. But when she realized it was like a thank-you present to the waitstaff, she'd slipped all her tips into the tip jar when Alice wasn't looking.

She didn't think she'd contributed enough to turn business around. But maybe it was a start.

The rest of the day passed uneventfully. Olivia came by after school, with the same friends dropping her off outside. The four held another whispered conference before she went inside.

That night, Piper was exhausted. All she wanted to do was sleep. But even in the dark, she could tell Olivia's eyes were wide open and staring at the ceiling. The girl was afraid to fall asleep.

"Do you think you can talk me through that relaxation technique again?" Olivia asked almost shyly.

"I could," Piper agreed, "but there's another approach we can try, too." *And maybe this one will work better,* she added to herself. "Close your eyes, and imagine you're at the ocean." She stopped. "Wait a minute," she said to Olivia. "Do you even like the beach?"

"Love it," Olivia murmured.

"Okay, so you're standing on warm, smooth sand, looking out over the water. A light breeze ruffles your hair."

Piper thought she saw Olivia's hair lift slightly from her pillow.

"It's perfect," Piper went on, "except that you're holding a heavy backpack you can't put down, because you're afraid the tide will wash it away."

Olivia's shoulders hunched.

"Now each time a wave rolls onto the sand, one item disappears from your backpack. After it leaves, you feel stronger, less worried. Here comes the first wave . . . in . . . and . . . out."

Olivia's shoulders rose the slightest bit.

"And another wave . . . in . . . and . . . out, coming a little closer to your feet."

Each wave seemed to make Olivia's load lighter. Each wave came a little closer. Finally, Piper told Olivia she was carrying nothing at all, and the water lapped at her feet, cleansing and purifying her mind.

Olivia sighed happily. "Thank you, Piper."

"You're welcome, Olivia. But I'll tell you something else that can make you feel better."

Olivia shifted to face her, still interested. "What?"

"Opening up to others." Piper held up a hand before Olivia could protest. "Opening up to people you trust can be a powerful force." She felt sure that was one reason Olivia had bad dreams: she was holding all her worries inside, not telling a soul. And they were finding their way into her dreams.

"There is strength in vulnerability," Piper went on, "and communicating emotions. It gives me so much energy I glow. . . . I mean, I feel like I'm glowing. It would make you feel energized and strong."

Piper waited patiently. She knew Olivia was mulling this over. And maybe, just maybe, she'd confide in Piper. She'd talk about her concerns about the diner. Then they could come up with a solution together.

When Olivia stayed quiet, Piper decided to change direction a bit. Maybe Olivia wanted to talk about the nightmares first.

"And you know what else? Dreams are amazing windows into feelings," she began. "They seem so real, because the emotions that drive them are real."

"And the feelings are intense!" Olivia put in. "They're even stronger than when I'm awake, because—"

"Your dream is so much more intense!"

"That's it exactly!" Olivia said. "I mean, I can dream I'm in school, but the next moment I'm climbing Mount Everest. In real life, when I'm in school, I'm in school, and I can't blink and find myself anywhere else."

Piper thought a moment. With enough wish energy manipulation practice, she could probably teleport from Halo Hall to the Crystal Mountains in the middle of Astral Accounting class. But it didn't seem right to mention it to Olivia. Besides, she understood exactly what Olivia meant.

"Dreams make the impossible possible," she said. "So they can be amazing and crazy and scary and wonderful all at the same time. Believe me, I know how powerful dreams can be. But you're going to wake up. They can never really hurt you. In fact, they may be able to help you. They have meaning and can guide you."

"Grandma Rosie used to say something like that, that dreams are the windows to the soul."

"She did?" Piper said, delighted. "I really wish I knew her."

A tear slid down Olivia's cheek. "I really miss her. My parents are great and everything, obviously. But they work crazy hours and in their downtime they have so many things to take care of, like taking me to the doctor, buying me shoes, helping me with my homework. . . ."

This didn't seem to have much to do with diner business. Still, Piper thought it could lead to a revelation. So she nodded, interested.

"My grandma and I would just talk and talk, especially once Isabel left for college and I was on my own so much. I could tell her anything. Good, bad, it didn't matter. She always understood." Olivia lowered her voice. "If she were here right now, I'd talk to her. I'd tell her—" She paused. Piper knew she was about to say something important, something revealing—something that would confirm Olivia's wish.

But for some reason, Piper had to finish Olivia's sentence: "That you're flailing around, worried about everything, trying to get through the nights when everything around you seems so dark and unforgiving."

Piper felt Olivia stiffen. And even in the darkness, she could see her face draw closed.

"I'm going to sleep now, Piper. Good night."

Piper groaned softly. She wished she hadn't been quite so gloomy and bleak. But sometimes she just couldn't help it.

CHAPTER
9

By the time Piper woke up, the sun was high in the sky. Olivia's bed was neatly made, the blanket stretched tight and tucked into the corners.

Piper wiggled her toes, then raised her arms over her head for an easy stretch. The clock on the nightstand read 11:19, late even by her standards. She heard some thumps and bumps and light steps coming down the hall.

That must be Olivia, she thought. *Good, I'm not alone.*

She hoped Olivia had been able to sleep late, too. It was Saturday. And as far as she knew, her Wisher hadn't needed to be anywhere early. Of course, there was the not-so-small matter of the Countdown Clock and starmins ticking away. The wish had to be granted by that evening. Still, Piper felt confident.

A nagging doubt tugged at the far corner of her mind. . . . Those feelings Olivia was about to talk about when Piper interrupted . . . they could have been important. Maybe they wouldn't have confirmed the wish. Maybe they would have pointed in an entirely different direction. But Piper shook away those negative thoughts. She had nailed down Olivia's wish: improving business. And they had all day at the diner to make it happen.

Moving a little more quickly than usual, Piper dressed with the help of her Wishworld Outfit Selector. She settled on stretchy black leggings and a shimmery seafoam green blouse that fell to her hips. Not her usual look, but it was both pretty and comfortable.

"Oh, good. You're ready," Olivia said, walking into the room just as Piper was letting the air out of the blow-up bed. "I told my parents we'd be at the diner around lunchtime to help."

Olivia was quiet as they walked to work. But it was a companionable silence. Piper was pleased. Clearly, Olivia had gotten past the previous night's irritation.

As they neared Big Rosie's, the two girls gasped.

"Oh, my stars!" Piper said. A line of customers stretched out the door. "What's going on?"

"I have no idea," Olivia answered. "Let's find out."

She led Piper to the entrance, skirting people she

knew. "Excuse us, Mr. Raymond. Hi, Thomas. Could you let us past?"

Inside, they saw some people waiting for tables, but many more were by the takeout counter.

"Two chocolate egg creams to go, and throw in a blueberry muffin," one woman said to Donna, the waitress who had called in sick the other day.

"Egg creams!" Olivia repeated. "How does she know about egg creams?"

Just then a customer sitting at a table flagged down Diane. "We'd like egg creams, too," he said.

"This is beyond weird," Olivia said as the next customer in line ordered an egg cream with a bagel.

Alice hurried to the girls. "Everyone wants egg creams!" she said excitedly. "Some are just ordering them at the counter. But lots are staying for full meals."

She put her hand on Piper's shoulder. "We're doing incredible business. Just look at all these people. Apparently one of our customers tweeted about our amazing egg creams with a photo."

"It must have been Sammy's dad," said Piper.

"It's all thanks to you," Alice told her.

"No, it wasn't me. It was really Olivia. She made it for me the other day, remember? Then I just suggested it to a customer." Piper gazed around the diner. Practically everybody had an egg cream. "It's really caught on."

"You know, I think we'll add it to the menu," Alice said. "In fact, we should come up with other new drinks. And maybe desserts." She smiled. "First on the list is that rhubarb pie I keep thinking about!"

"Yeah, but we don't have to stop there," Olivia said. "We can add dinner entrees and appetizers and—"

"The sky's the limit!" Piper broke in.

"Now hurry up and grab some aprons," Alice said. "Things will move more quickly with you two here."

"This is so amazing!" Olivia told Piper as they rushed to the back room. "All this business is really going to help my parents out."

Piper looked at Olivia. Her shoulders were relaxed and the furrow between her eyebrows was gone. This was it. She'd helped Olivia get her wish. She stood still, waiting for the wish energy to flow.

"What?" said Olivia. "Come on! Get moving! We have work to do!"

Still, Piper just stood there, staring at Olivia. Any starsec now a colorful wave would stream from her Wisher straight to her bracelet pendants.

Where were the sparks she had heard about? The rainbow of lights and flashes shooting out from Olivia to Piper? Piper was confused. But maybe the wish wasn't entirely granted yet. Maybe the energy would come later, when they waited on their fiftieth customer or reached a certain dollar amount.

"Okay, let's get cracking!" said Piper. This would be her very last shift. She wanted to make it a good—no, great!—one.

Hours passed in a blur. Customers kept coming and Piper kept working. But still no wish energy. Her shoulders sagged. What was the problem?

"Something wrong?" asked Olivia, stepping around her with a tray full of chocolate egg creams.

"Olivia," Piper said slowly. "Do you think business is booming? That you guys have enough customers now?"

"Of course!" Olivia said happily. "We've never been so busy!"

"So you're not thinking to yourself, 'Oh, it would be great if we reached nine hundred ninety-nine customers. Or if we made a million dollars'?" Piper wasn't actually sure if a million was a lot of dollars, but it sounded good.

"Uh, no. I think this is perfect!"

Olivia was thrilled with the business now. So, clearly, that hadn't been her wish at all.

Piper stared at Olivia despairingly. What could her wish be? She had wasted all that time on the wrong wish! Now she was running out of time. Wish identification was much more difficult than Piper had ever dreamed.

The crowd was thinning out. Piper began wiping down tables. Then the bell above the door jangled. She looked up to see Olivia's friends walking into the diner. When Piper stepped behind the counter, she could see straight to the door. Olivia's friends were just walking through.

Olivia walked in carrying a tray of ketchup dispensers she had just filled. When she spotted her friends, a shadow passed over Olivia's face. Oh, no, another blunder. Piper must have hurt Olivia's feelings, saying the girls were there for the food, not their friend. "No! I bet they're here just for you!"

Olivia watched as the girls took a table at the far end, her mouth tugging down at the corners. "I'll wait on them," she said, grabbing some menus. Seconds later, she stood at their table, whispering. Then she actually sat down next to the short girl, the one named Morgan. Piper had never seen her do that before!

"Olivia!" her dad called loudly. "Your sixteen with SPF and MG is ready."

Part of Piper couldn't help identifying what that meant—cheeseburger with sweet potato fries and mixed greens—even while she was concentrating on Olivia.

Reluctantly, Olivia got up, then walked slowly away from her friends.

Friends! The word hit Piper like a bolt of white-hot lightning.

Friendship must be as important to Olivia as the diner, maybe even more. Piper remembered her first wish identification guess, that Olivia was spending too much time at the diner. Maybe she'd been half right. Olivia loved working at the diner. But it still got in the way of her being with her friends.

Okay, Piper was sure she had it right this time: Olivia wished she could spend more time with her friends.

Without waiting another starmin, Piper grabbed a bag of candy, then refilled the FREE MINTS bowl by the cash register. "You know," she said to Alice, looking deep into her eyes, "Olivia should have the night off, and have those friends"—she pointed to the table—"plus me, over for a sleepover."

"You know," Alice said thoughtfully, "I think Olivia should have the night off, and have those friends—plus you—over for a sleepover. Diane can stay late."

"I'll tell Olivia!" Piper said. She grabbed the girl's hand and pulled her back to the table. "Hey!" she said to the girls. Morgan, the short one who Piper thought might be bossy, looked up. The girl sitting next to her was Ruby. She nodded hello, her shoulder-length hair bouncing. The third girl was Chase and she had bright green braces that showed when she smiled at Piper. "Alice said we can all have a slumber party at Olivia's tonight."

"And who are you?" asked Morgan, sounding just shy of rude.

"This is Piper," said Olivia. "I told you, she's been staying with us while she works on a school project."

Everyone seemed to wait for Morgan to respond. Finally, she shrugged, saying, "Sure, sounds like fun."

"It will be!" Piper assured her. "We can have a dream slumber party! We'll decorate notebooks with glitter or stickers or any way we like to make dream journals! Then in the morning we can write down our dreams. Any dreams," she hastened to add. "From the night before or the week before, good or bad."

Piper plowed on, not waiting for a reaction. "Maybe I can help you guys figure out what your dreams mean." She looked down modestly. "I have a knack for dream interpretation."

Again, everyone waited for Morgan, Piper with bated breath. She had to like the idea. It was nothing short of brilliant, if Piper did say so herself. The sleepover activity could help grant Olivia's wish *and* serve as a healing session, to clear Olivia's mind of any disturbing thoughts. All at the same time!

Morgan tilted her head, thinking it over. "That's cool," she finally said.

Immediately, the two other girls agreed, and the three began chattering about what to bring.

"No!" Olivia interrupted them, her voice rising above the others. Everyone stopped talking and looked at her, surprised. "I mean, it sounds great. Really. But we can't do it. I have to—"

"Work tonight? Don't worry!" Piper said gleefully. "I already spoke to your mom. She's totally fine with it. Diane's going to fill in."

Morgan, Ruby, and Chase started talking again and took out their cell phones to ask permission. Meanwhile, Piper gazed anxiously at Olivia. She had thought Olivia would be thrilled her friends were coming over. Instead, she didn't seem any happier than she had earlier. In fact, her expression was downright glum.

Olivia edged away from her friends to talk to Diane. "I'm sorry you have to take my shift," she told her.

Oh, so that was it. Olivia felt bad that Diane was working extra hours. That was why she wasn't excited— yet. Piper felt sure that once the girls actually came to her house, everything would change.

According to the Countdown Clock, the wish had to be granted that evening, by eight o'clock. Piper's pulse quickened. She'd have to return to Starland—with or without Olivia's wish energy. Already she could feel her own energy level sinking. She'd been there so long and accomplished so little. . . .

Piper shook her head to clear it and envisioned a smiling Olivia radiating a rainbow of colored light. It could happen. It *would* happen. If only Piper didn't feel so tired . . .

"Table number two is wobbly," Diane said, hurrying past. "Do you think you could fix it?"

"Of course," said Piper, straightening up. She was putting a piece of cardboard under one table leg to keep it steady when the bells above the door jingled, signaling another customer. Piper felt a tingle run down her spine. She froze, her head still under the table. Something was about to change. She heard a familiar voice: "Oh, so this is a diner."

It was Astra! In her haste to actually see a fellow Star Darling, Piper stood up without thinking. "Ouch!" she said, banging her head.

Piper sighed. This wouldn't do at all. She had to center herself, concentrate on unhurried action and calm movement.

She took a breath and came out from under the table in one fluid motion. "Astra!" she called, beaming happily as she saw her friend in her glittery glory. She knew that she looked sparkly to Astra, too, and that made her feel good. She felt so glad to see someone who knew all about her, even if it meant Lady Stella thought she needed help. And while Piper thought she had matters well in hand, another Star Darling could only be helpful.

Astra was wearing a sporty outfit, cutoffs, red sneakers, and a T-shirt with a red star on it. Her hair, now a flaming auburn, was pulled into two pigtails. She looked friendly and confident, a girl any Wishling would want as a friend.

Alice stood by the cash register, smiling at the girls. "Hi . . . Astra?" she said questioningly. Piper nodded. "Are you a friend of Piper's?"

"Yes," said Astra. "We go to the same school." She was looking around, soaking in all the sights and sounds and smells. It was a little mind-blowing when you first got there, Piper knew. So much was similar to Starland, but so much was different. "Your world is amazing," she told Alice.

Luckily, Alice said, "Yes, the diner is my world, along with my family, of course. You must be from Maylefield, too."

"Maylefield," repeated Astra, sounding as if she'd never heard of it before, which, of course, she hadn't.

"Yup," said Piper, linking her arm through Astra's. "She just came for a visit."

Astra nodded, finally realizing she had to be more careful. "Let me fill you in on what's been going on in . . . uh . . . Maylefield, Piper."

She pulled Piper aside, adding, "Star apologies for being a little dense. There's just so much to take in." She turned toward the cash register, fascinated when the cash drawer sprung open.

"Is everything okay at home?" Piper asked as they found two empty seats at the counter.

"Things haven't gotten any better," Astra told her. "There've been more power flickers. I'm not sure anyone outside Starling Academy has been paying attention, though. But, Piper, you must know why I'm here. Lady Stella thought you could use some help."

"I do know." Piper was actually quite glad Astra was there. Her presence gave Piper a personal energy lift. "Let me introduce you to Olivia, my Wisher."

Of course Astra made a good impression; she even made Olivia smile when she asked about her favorite item at the diner.

"Well, you won't find it on the menu yet, but it's the chocolate egg cream."

While Olivia performed her magic roll-ups, Piper

made Astra an egg cream and quickly filled her in on Olivia, the diner, and the sleepover.

Astra listened, picking up a nearby saltshaker. "What is this thing?" she asked.

"Wishlings use it to season their food," said Piper. "Dishes don't come out perfectly like the food at home."

Astra sipped her egg cream. "Starmazing!" she proclaimed. "And totally worth the trip."

Just then the customer sitting next to Astra picked up the saltshaker and shook it over her French fries. The shaker top fell off, and all the salt rained down on her food.

"Oh, no!" she gasped.

Piper took the plate from the customer. "I'll just get you another serving," she said. "On the house."

While Piper was getting more fries, she stopped to talk to Alice and get Astra invited to the sleepover, too. When she returned, Astra was spinning on the stool.

"You are officially invited to Olivia's sleepover," she told her. "To watch me collect my wish energy!"

"I can't wait," said Astra. "But do you really think it's going to be that easy? I mean, why am I here?"

Piper shook her head. "It's all under control, Astra," she said.

CHAPTER
10

Olivia still wasn't excited about the sleepover, but Alice certainly was. For the first time in a long while, she left the diner early. "Just to get a few things for the party," she told the girls.

By the time Piper, Astra, and Olivia got to the house, it was filled with slumber party supplies. "It's not every day we host a party at home," Alice told Olivia. "I want to make it special for you."

Olivia scanned the food, crafts, balloons, and decorations. "This is all for tonight?" she asked. "Or are we starting a party business?"

"No business tonight," Alice said. "You've been working too hard—at the diner and at school. And you just did so well on that history test. I'm proud of you, honey. Consider this a reward."

Olivia flushed. "I'm going to change," she said, hurrying out of the room.

Alice frowned. "I just want to make this a fun night," she said. "I want Olivia to have a good time." She sighed, looking down at a stack of plain white pillowcases, ready to be decorated with fabric markers. "And I might have gone a little overboard."

Piper glanced around the room. She was glad to see that Alice remembered the dream journals, too.

"Piper and I can set all this up," Astra offered.

"Thanks," said Alice. "That will give me time to make dinner and dessert."

Alice left for the kitchen, and Piper and Astra sorted through the stuff.

The two agreed that play stations, kind of like workstations at the diner, would be fun. So they pushed tables here and there, made signs, and artfully arranged the supplies.

When Olivia returned, she looked no more enthusiastic than she had earlier. Piper gazed at her anxiously as Olivia took stock of the living room. There was a mani/pedi station and a decorate-your-own-pillowcase table next to a spot with mason jars and glow-in-the-dark paint. When they were done painting the jars, they'd look like colorful lanterns. All perfect for a slumber party, Piper thought.

"We're not done decorating yet," she told Olivia. "Let's make glitter balloons to hang around the room."

The three girls blew up balloons and dipped them in glue, followed by glitter.

"They look like sparkly disco balls," Olivia said, looking pleased. Standing on chairs, the girls hung them upside down from the ceiling.

Inspired, Olivia ran to the attic and returned with twinkle lights. Working together, the girls strung them from room to room.

Olivia's spirits seemed to be rising. Piper took this as a good sign that she had identified the right wish. But she wanted to make sure. "Isn't this great, that you get to spend so much time with friends? Like a wish come true?"

Olivia shrugged, twisting a lightbulb so it turned on. The light cast a rosy glow over her face. "Yeah, it's okay they're coming over. It'll be nice. But a wish come true? I wouldn't go quite that far."

Piper felt a sinking feeling in her stomach, as if she'd taken an express ride in the Flash Vertical Mover. She slid over to whisper the news to Astra: she had the wrong wish again! And the girls exchanged worried glances just as the doorbell rang.

Piper stole a glance at the Countdown Clock. Three hours and fourteen minutes remaining! Could she figure it out in time? Morgan, Ruby, and Chase tumbled in all at once, laughing and talking, oohing and aahing over the decorations and party ideas. Piper moved to the music station and picked out music to play. With Astra's help, she figured out how to work the device. Soon a soothing instrumental piece filled the room.

Piper snuck away to a mirror in the front hall and chanted her Mirror Mantra one more time. "You can do it, Piper," she said to her reflection. And somehow, it boosted her mood.

Smiling, she rejoined the group.

The evening was filled with activities. They had breakfast for dinner, with the girls throwing their own veggies and fillings into an omelet pan while Alice flipped the eggs. They played Truth or Dare, a game in which they had to answer an embarrassing question or take on a dare. Piper laughed when Astra wound up standing outside with a sign reading HONK IF YOU THINK I'M CUTE. She stopped laughing when she saw Astra tape the sign to the back of the shirt Morgan was planning to wear the next day. Chances were Morgan would see it before she wore it outside. But to be on the safe side, Piper tore it off.

Then Morgan suggested they give each other mani/pedis. She actually looked to Piper for confirmation, and Piper nodded, pleased.

Piper picked up a bottle of nail polish. It was a deeper green than the seafoam color she was wearing, and she thought she'd give it a try.

She glanced around for a nail polish remover machine, then realized the other girls were removing their old polish with liquid from a bottle. She, too, soaked a ball of fluff in the harsh liquid and rubbed her nails. Astra joined her. "It's cold," said Piper.

"It's not coming off," Astra said.

"It is really sticking," Piper agreed. "We'll just have to scrub harder."

The girls rubbed furiously. Finally, the color lightened a bit. "Keep at it," Piper urged. By the time the polish had come off completely, Piper's wrists ached from the effort. But it was worth it once she had the new polish on. The new green color looked lovely. She felt a bit lighter, too; with just a little more energy than before, she was ready for the next part of the plan. Would it help make the wish come true? Only time would tell.

She had the girls put on pajamas, then set up their

sleeping bags in the center of Olivia's room. They were spread in a star shape, with their heads in the center, just like the Star Darlings had been at Libby's.

They all looked at Piper expectantly. "Let's do some happy daydreaming," she said. Maybe it would lead to Olivia's revealing the real wish.

"What's that?" asked Morgan.

"You just close your eyes and picture a place in your mind—a place that makes you happier than any other. It can be somewhere you'd like to go or a place you'd like to visit, real or not. It could be your room, just like it is, or made entirely of candy." She searched her brain for Wishling examples. "Marshmallow pillows, fruit strips for blankets, candy bar chairs . . ."

"My happy place is on the playing field," said Astra.

"Really?" Morgan humphed.

"Come on," Piper gently admonished. "There is no wrong place to set a happy daydream. Astra's may be different from yours, but the point is to open yourself to positive feelings. It's very personal." She thought a moment. "My happy place is a sparkling stream, a place I can do the back float, with stars twinkling above."

"I like to swim, too," Ruby said. "But my happy place is the ocean, where I can dive down deep to meet dolphins and ride on their backs and"—she stood with a little pirouette—"maybe perform water ballet with them, too."

"My happy place is my grandma's kitchen," Olivia said quietly. "With the smell of freshly baked cookies and my grandma about to pour a big cold glass of milk for me. All the smells are mixing together: the cookies, the flowers she always kept in a blue vase, her perfume . . ." Her voice trailed off as she closed her eyes and smiled dreamily.

Piper closed her eyes, too. "Isn't that wonderful? And you can go to these places anytime you want. You just have to picture it and feel the joy."

Piper felt more relaxed than she had all day, and she sensed the girls felt the same. Now was the time to uncover Olivia's real wish.

"You know," Piper continued, "happy daydreaming can carry over into your nighttime dreams. They can help make them sweet and pleasant. But even bad dreams have their place."

"I don't like bad dreams," Olivia said, shaking her head. "And I don't see why anyone would."

"Well, bad dreams have meaning. And they're not necessarily literal. If you're dreaming you're stuck in a glion's—I mean, lion's—cage, of course you aren't really there. But you can discover something from the dream, like maybe you're afraid of your neighbor's pet."

"Tell us one of your nightmares," Morgan suggested.

"Okay." Piper thought a moment. "Once I dreamed I was on a Flash Vertical . . . I mean, elevator . . . and I kept going up and up and up, which was fine. I wanted to get to the top floor. But each time I looked, the floor numbers changed—they kept going higher, and so I had to go higher and higher, too, or I would never get off. It was scary, sure. But I realized what it meant: I was waiting to hear if I got accepted to the school where Astra and I go, and if I didn't get in—reach the top—I'd be stuck forever. Or at least that's how I felt. It made me realize how important school was to me."

At the word *school*, Piper noticed Olivia sneaking a furtive look at her desk. Maybe it meant something; maybe it didn't. But Piper decided to use her special sun-ray vision talent to look inside.

All she saw were pencils, old gum wrapped in tissues, and a crumpled-up paper. It looked like a test, with questions and answers and, in the corner, a grade: A. *That must be a terrible grade*, she thought, *for Olivia to crumple it up like that.*

But then she remembered the customer talking about Isabel's As and how great they were. So A was good. Why did Olivia have a problem with that?

"I understand what you mean, Piper," Olivia was saying softly. "I have this same dream again and again where I'm chewing gum or eating candy, and at first it's great. But then the gum—or whatever—keeps getting bigger and bigger and fills my whole mouth. I want to scream or shout for help, but I can't talk, and I can't tell anyone what's wrong. I feel like I can't breathe, and then I wake up shaking."

Again, she stole a look at the drawer.

"It probably doesn't sound so awful. I mean, I'm eating candy! But it is. When I wake up, I have this sickeningly sweet taste in my—"

"Mouth," said Piper. She swallowed in sympathy. She could almost taste it, too, a cloying sugary sensation clogging up her throat. "When did you start having this dream?" she asked gently. Olivia was finally opening up. And if they could figure out more about the dream, it might just reveal the wish.

"Two weeks ago. I remember it was a Thursday night, because I was so rattled I forgot to wear sneakers to school the next morning. And that's when we have gym."

"That was just after we saw Another World," Morgan added.

"You traveled to another world?" Astra asked unbelievingly. She shot a look at Piper to say, *And we thought Wishlings were so primitive!*

"I know, it's unbelievable! But we didn't have to go far. They were playing in the next town over."

Ruby sighed. "That band is the best thing I've ever seen."

"Oh," Piper couldn't help saying. Another World was a group, and the girls had gone to their concert.

"I was exhausted at school the next day," Ruby went on. "And we had that test!"

"But it all worked out," Morgan said.

Piper thought hard. Olivia kept having nightmares in which she couldn't talk. And she'd stayed out late the night before that history test. That had to be connected to her wish.

She reached over and pulled open the desk drawer. "Don't!" Olivia cried. But before she could stop her, Piper took out the test. " 'Great job, Olivia,' " she read from the top. "Has this test been on your mind?" she asked.

Olivia sighed and slowly nodded. "Yes, we had this big history test scheduled for the day after the concert.

I never told my parents about it. They wouldn't have let me go if they knew."

"And we didn't have time to study," Chase added.

The four girls looked at each other in silence. They seemed miserable. Finally, Morgan nodded. "We didn't know what to do," Olivia started. "We knew we'd fail the test and we were scared. So we wrote up cheat sheets the day before," she said slowly. "And we all got As."

Olivia looked down. "I hate to disappoint my parents about grades. They expect me to do as well as Isabel! Still, I wish I hadn't cheated. It feels—"

"Awful," said Piper, nodding.

The wish! Her heartbeat quickened. But she couldn't grant that wish. She couldn't go back in time. But that dream where Olivia couldn't speak . . .

"I bet you'd feel better if you told your mother the truth," she said to Olivia.

"I wish I could!" Olivia said quickly. "But I'd get everyone else in trouble, too. And these guys don't want to get in trouble!" She shrugged. "So it's done."

So that was what the four had been whispering about, and why Olivia wasn't thrilled to be spending time with them now.

"You know, it must be bothering me, too," said Ruby.

"I've been having weird dreams about Ms. Stadler following me home from school."

"Me three," said Chase. "I had a nightmare that I had to go to a special summer school for cheaters."

The girls turned to Morgan. Piper knew she was the one holding the others back. "Just imagine how much better you'd all feel after talking about this," Piper said. "You'd be able to connect to your happy daydreams without a pesky nightmare getting in the way."

Morgan jumped up. "Okay! I'm sorry I've been such an idiot about the whole thing. I was just scared. Let's tell the whole world we cheated!"

"Well, I don't know if you have to do that." Piper grinned. "Olivia, why don't we start with your mom?"

Morgan, Chase, and Ruby followed Olivia to the kitchen. "Mom," Olivia said, "I have something to tell you."

Piper stood around the corner. She held out her wrist just as the wish energy whipped around the wall, straight into her pendant. And just in time, too. She and Astra grinned at each other.

Astra and Piper decided they'd leave in the morning. Exhausted, the girls all climbed back into their sleeping bags.

Alice had been disappointed, but proud of the girls for telling the truth. Piper could feel the relief coming from Olivia. She squeezed Piper's hand. "Thank you for helping me tell the truth," she said. Piper squeezed back.

The next morning, Piper was the last to wake up—again. She found the girls and Astra eating waffles in the kitchen. Morgan, Chase, and Ruby decided they would tell their parents later that day and they would go to their teacher together on Monday morning.

Piper was pleased to note that everyone looked well rested. "I slept like a baby," Olivia said delightedly.

It was almost time to leave. But Piper wanted to do one more sleepover activity. "Let's write in our dream journals!" she told the girls.

As the Wishlings bent their heads over their notebooks, recording their dreams, Piper and Astra smiled and nodded at each other.

A little while later, Morgan glanced at her phone and slammed her book shut. "My mom is picking us up in ten minutes," she announced.

"Astra and I have to leave, too," Piper told Olivia. "I've certainly been here long enough!"

Olivia grinned. "It's been great, Piper. And you can visit anytime. My mom said you could even work at the diner over the summer!"

The girls gathered their things and headed outside. Piper took a long last look at Olivia, who was chatting happily to her friends. It would have been fun to hang out with Olivia and work at the diner. But she had another job to finish.

"Well, good-bye, Olivia," she said, feeling her eyes fill with tears.

"Don't look so sad," said Olivia. "We'll see each other soon."

She hugged Piper close, and when she pulled away, she looked at her blankly. The hug had erased all memories of the Star Darlings.

"Oh, hi!" said Piper. "Can you give my friend and me directions to the train station? I have to catch the next train home."

"Sure," said Olivia, pointing. "Walk two blocks, then turn left." Just then a minivan pulled up to the curb, and Olivia disappeared into a happy huddle with her friends.

"Are you ready to head home?" Astra asked Piper as they walked away. "We need to find an out-of-the-way place to unfold our stars and shoot back home."

Piper nodded. She was ready.

Epilogue

It was a smooth ride home from Wishworld, much easier than the trip there. Piper somehow landed on the shore of Luminous Lake, where she took a few moments to close her eyes, relive her journey, and put herself back in the Starland mind-set.

Just as Piper opened her eyes, her Star-Zap flashed. "I landed right behind the dorms," Astra holo-texted. "So everyone knows about your mission already. Come to Lady Stella's office right now for a meeting."

Even though she'd hurried about the diner, Piper still didn't like to rush. But she did put a little energy into moving quickly. She had successfully completed her mission, after all. And the ceremony was special. She couldn't wait to see if her Wish Blossom had a gemstone inside.

Everyone was already at the office when Piper got there. When she walked in, the Star Darlings stood and clapped.

"Congratulations!" Vega cried. "You did great. And here you are, not even late!"

Clover quickly stepped up, giving Piper a hug. Then she went from Starling to Starling, hugging each one, including Scarlet, who couldn't pull away fast enough.

Still, Scarlet smiled, skipping over to Piper to offer her own congratulations.

Libby said nothing. As soon as she'd sat down, she'd fallen asleep.

Lady Stella entered the room. "Welcome back, Piper," she said. "You did a startastic job!"

Piper smiled broadly and shimmered with pride.

"Now you should all take a seat," the headmistress continued.

Gemma lifted a chair. "Um . . . where should I take it?"

Piper suddenly felt very tired. There was a weird tension in the air that left her feeling uneasy. She looked over at Astra, who had a puzzled expression on her face.

Then Lady Stella stepped forward, Piper's Wish Blossom cupped in her hands. As Piper reached to accept it, it began to glow brighter and brighter. Piper gasped as it started to transform. "Why, it's a sleepibelle!" Piper whispered, delighted. She loved the way its hanging petals swung in a soothing motion, back and forth like a pendulum. It's soothing glow warmed her right to her toes. Then, one by one, its drooping petals rose and unfurled. And there was her Power Crystal. "Dreamalite," Lady Stella declared.

Gingerly, Piper picked up the stone, sparkling green with hidden depths. Holding it felt right. It touched Piper's very essence. This was a stone she would never, ever lose.

Lady Stella nodded seriously, then continued. "I know it's been an unsettling few days here."

Sage giggled.

"So it's extra nice to have Piper—and Astra—back safely from a mission well done."

Once again, the Star Darlings applauded.

As Sage tried to pull Libby to her feet and everyone started to leave, Astra edged closer to Piper. "Is it me," she asked, "or is something different?"

"It's not you," Piper said. "I think so, too. Maybe it took us going away to see it."

Something was not quite right. But what in the stars was it?

Glossary

Afterglow: The Starling afterlife. When Starlings die, it is said that they have "begun their afterglow."

Age of fulfillment: The age when a Starling is considered mature enough to begin to study wish granting.

Bad Wish Orbs: Orbs that are the result of bad or selfish wishes made on Wishworld. These grow dark and warped and are quickly sent to the Negative Energy Facility.

Ballum blossom tree: A Starland tree with cherry blossom–like flowers that light up at night.

Big Dipper Dormitory: Where third- and fourth-year students live.

Bot-Bot: A Starland robot. There are Bot-Bot guards, waiters, deliverers, and guides on Starland.

Bright Day: The date a Starling is born, celebrated each year like a Wishling birthday.

Celestial Café: Starling Academy's outstanding cafeteria.

Cocomoon: A sweet and creamy fruit with an iridescent glow.

Cosmic Transporter: The moving sidewalk system that transports students through dorms and across the Starling Academy campus.

Countdown Clock: A timing device on a Starling's Star-Zap. It lets them know how much time is left on a Wish Mission, which coincides with when the Wish Orb will fade.

Crystal Mountains: The most beautiful mountains on Starland. They are located across the lake from Starling Academy.

Cycle of Life: A Starling's life span. When Starlings die, they are said to have "completed their Cycle of Life."

Dramboozle: A natural herb that promotes sweet dreams and comforting sleep.

Druderwomp: An edible barrel-like bush capable of pulling up its own roots and rolling like a tumbleweed, then planting itself again.

Flareworks: Colorful displays at the Festival of Illumination.

Flutterfocus: A Starland creature similar to a Wishworld butterfly but with illuminated wings.

Galliope: A sparkly Starland creature similar to a Wishworld horse.

Garble greens: A Starland vegetable similar to spinach.

Glimmerwillow tree: A Starland tree with hanging branches called glimmervines that create a space at its base resembling a closed-off leafy room.

Glitterberries: A sweet Starland fruit.

Gloak tree: A Starland tree known for its strength and beauty.

Globerbeem: Large, friendly lightning bug–type insects that are sparkly and lay eggs.

Gloom flats: A rural, sparsely populated, dimly illuminated area of Starland and home to Piper's family.

Glorange: A glowing orange fruit. Its juice is often enjoyed at breakfast time.

Glowfur: A small, furry Starland creature with gossamer wings that eats flowers and glows.

Glowmoss: A soft vegetation that covers fields on Starland.

Good Wish Orbs: Orbs that are the result of positive wishes made on Wishworld. They are planted in Wish-Houses.

Halo Hall: The building where Starling Academy classes are held.

Holo-text: A message received on a Star-Zap and projected into the air. There are also holo-albums, holo-billboards, holo-books, holo-cards, holo-communications, holo-diaries, holo-flyers, holo-letters, holo-papers, holo-pictures, and holo–place cards. Anything that would be made of paper or contain writing or images on Wishworld is a hologram on Starland.

Hydrong: The equivalent of a Wishworld hundred.

Impossible Wish Orbs: Orbs that are the result of wishes made on Wishworld that are beyond the power of Starlings to grant.

Isle of Misera: A barren rocky island off the coast of New Prism.

Lightku: A spare and simple poem with only three lines of verse and seventeen syllables total.

Lightku Isle: An isolated part of Starland with sandy, sparkling beaches, where local Starlings speak solely in lightkus.

Lightning Lounge: A place on the Starling Academy campus where students relax and socialize.

Little Dipper Dormitory: Where first- and second-year students live.

Luminous Lake: A serene and lovely lake next to the Starling Academy campus.

Luminous Library: The impressive library at Starling Academy.

Mirror Mantra: A saying specific to each Star Darling that when recited gives her (and her Wisher) reassurance and strength. When a Starling recites her Mirror Mantra while looking in a mirror, she will see her true appearance reflected.

Moonium: An amount similar to a Wishworld million.

Old Prism: A medium-sized historical city about an hour from Starling Academy.

Plinking: A delicious striped fruit that bounces like a ball.

Power Crystal: The powerful stone that each Star Darling receives once she has granted her first wish.

Serenity Islands: A Starland recreation area. Starlings sometimes take hover-canoe rides around it.

Shooting stars: Speeding stars that Starlings can latch on to and ride to Wishworld.

Silver Blossom: The final manifestation of a Good Wish Orb. This glimmering metallic bloom is placed in the Hall of Granted Wishes.

Sleepibelle: Piper's Wish Blossom. Its blue-green petals hang down and swing in a soothing motion, like a pendulum.

Snuggle sack: A heavily quilted tube that immediately adjusts to a Starling's height and body shape for extreme comfort.

Sparklecorn: A versatile Starland food.

Sparkle shower: An energy shower Starlings take every day to get clean and refresh their sparkling glow.

Star ball: An intramural sport that shares similarities with soccer on Wishworld. But star ball players use energy manipulation to control the ball.

Starcar: The primary mode of transportation for most Starlings. These ultrasafe vehicles drive themselves on cushions of wish energy.

Star Caves: The caverns underneath Starling Academy where the Star Darlings' secret Wish-Cavern is located.

Starf!: A Starling expression of dismay.

Star flash: News bulletin, often used starcastically.

Star Kindness Day: A special Starland holiday that celebrates spreading kindness, compliments, and good cheer.

Starland City: The largest city on Starland, also its capital.

Starlicious: Tasty, delicious.

Starlings: The glowing beings with sparkly skin who live on Starland.

Starpepper jelly: A condiment (often crushed) that adds spice and flavor to Starland foods.

Star Quad: The center of the Starling Academy campus. The dancing fountain, band shell, and hedge maze are located here.

Star sack: A Starland tote bag. This container starts about the size of a lunch bag, but it expands to hold whatever is stored inside.

Star salutations: The Starling way to say "thank you."

Staryear: A period of 365 days on Starland, the equivalent of a Wishworld year.

Star-Zap: The ultimate smartphone that Starlings use for all communications. It has myriad features.

Stellar School: A rival of Starling Academy in star ball.

Stellation: The point of a star. Halo Hall has five stellations, each housing a different department.

Sunnet: A rhyming poem that can be any length and meter but must include a source of light.

Supernova: A stellar explosion. Also used colloquially, meaning "really angry," as in "She went supernova when she found out the bad news."

Time of Letting Go: One of the four seasons on Starland. It falls between the warmest season and the coldest, similar to fall on Wishworld.

Time of Lumiere: The warmest season on Starland, similar to summer on Wishworld.

Time of New Beginnings: Similar to spring on Wishworld, this is the season that follows the coldest time of year; it's when plants and trees come into bloom.

Time of Shadows: The coldest season of the year on Starland, similar to winter on Wishworld.

Toothlight: A high-tech gadget that Starlings use to clean their teeth.

Trilight: A planet with three moons that is visible from Starland.

Wish Blossom: The bloom that appears from a Wish Orb after its wish is granted.

Wish energy: The positive energy that is released when a wish is granted. Wish energy powers everything on Starland.

Wisher: The Wishling who has made the wish that is being granted.

Wish-Granters: Starlings whose job is to travel down to Wishworld to help make wishes come true and collect wish energy.

Wish-House: The place where Wish Orbs are planted and cared for until they sparkle. Once the orb's wish is granted, it becomes a Wish Blossom.

Wishlings: The inhabitants of Wishworld.

Wish Mission: The task a Starling undertakes when she travels to Wishworld to help grant a wish.

Wish Orb: The form a wish takes on Wishworld before traveling to Starland. There it will grow and sparkle when it's time to grant the wish.

Wish Pendant: A gadget that absorbs and transports wish energy, helps Starlings locate their Wishers, and changes a Starling's appearance. Each Wish Pendant holds a different special power for its Star Darling.

Wishworld: The planet Starland relies on for wish energy. The beings on Wishworld know it by another name—Earth.

Wishworld Outfit Selector: A program on each Star-Zap that accesses Wishworld fashions for Starlings to wear to blend in on their Wish Missions.

Wishworld Surveillance Deck: Located high above the campus, it is where Starling Academy students go to observe Wishlings through high-powered telescopes.

Zing: A traditional Starling breakfast drink. It can be enjoyed hot or iced.

Shana Muldoon Zappa is a jewelry designer and writer who was born and raised in Los Angeles. She has an endless imagination and a passion to inspire positivity through her many artistic endeavors. She and her husband, Ahmet Zappa, collaborated on Star Darlings especially for their magical little girl and biggest inspiration, Halo Violetta Zappa.

Ahmet Zappa is the *New York Times* best-selling author of *Because I'm Your Dad* and *The Monstrous Memoirs of a Mighty McFearless*. He writes and produces films and television shows and loves pancakes, unicorns, and making funny faces for Halo and Shana.

Astra's Mixed-Up Mission

"Piper! Piper!" called Astra, waving urgently at the girl sitting across the cafeteria table from her. Astra's red-and-silver-striped fingernails caught the light and she noticed with dismay that the polish she had applied on Wishworld was already starting to chip. She knew it wouldn't last through her star ball practice later that afternoon. What a difference from her Starland manicure, which had taken *forever* to remove!

Piper looked up from her dream holo-diary, flipping a lock of hair the color of ocean foam over her shoulder. "Is someone on their way?" she asked.

"I think Tessa is heading over," Astra told her. When the two girls had returned from Piper's Wish Mission, they had immediately noticed that something seemed off with their fellow Star Darlings. Everyone was acting really odd. But they couldn't quite put their finger on exactly what was going on. So they decided they'd study their roommates first and report back to each other.

Back in their room, after Clover had hugged Astra tightly for the tenth time, Astra realized that no one could have possibly missed her that much. So she sent this holo-text:

 Clover is a mad hugger! What about Vega?

After a while she received the following holo-text:

 To figure it out took me some time. But Vega only talks in rhyme!

They made plans to study the rest of the Star Darlings the next starday, starting at breakfast. So there they sat, awaiting the other Starlings' arrival.

Piper shut off the holo-diary with a swipe of her hand. "Star apologies, Astra," she said. "I just thought I'd skim through some of my latest dream entries to see if I could come up with any clues about what's going on. You know, any themes or symbols that might have deeper meaning."

Just a few stardays ago Astra would have scoffed at such a statement. But now she totally got it. To be completely honest, when she first met Piper she found her slow dreaminess annoying and her occasional dark side ridiculous. But now Astra had a new respect both for the hidden messages that dreams could hold as well as the strength of Piper's intuitive powers. She also admired Piper's faith in herself. She didn't seem to care much about what others thought of her—much like Astra, in fact. Astra realized they had more similarities than they had differences and now they were fast friends. The fact that they both recognized that something was amiss had cemented their bond.

"Find anything?" Astra asked hopefully.

Piper sighed. "Not yet," she said.

They both watched as Tessa made a glitterbeeline for the table near the windows that the Star Darlings had claimed as their own, her brilliant green eyes flashing. All the Star Darlings knew how much Tessa loved food and looked forward to each meal. "Star greetings," she said pleasantly. She plopped down in a chair across from the two girls. "I'm starving!" she announced.

A Bot-Bot waiter zoomed up to drop off Piper's and Astra's breakfasts and take Tessa's order. She thought for a moment then nodded. "I'll take a pastry basket and a cup of Zing, please," she said.

Her breakfast arrived shortly thereafter and Tessa hovered her hand over the baked treats, licking her lips in anticipation. She pulled out an ozziefruit croissant and took a big bite. "Moonberry," she said when she was done chewing. She made quick work of the flaky pastry, then, dabbing the corners of her mouth with a cloth napkin for any errant crumbs, reached in again. This time she grabbed a mini moonmuffin, which Astra could see was liberally studded with lolofruit. She popped the entire thing into her mouth and chewed. "Moonberry again!" she said. "What are the chances?"

Astra's Star-Zap, which was sitting in her lap in silent mode, flickered. She flipped it open and read the message.

 Tessa = Everything tastes like moonberries?

 Sure looks that way!

Cassie and Sage strolled in next. Cassie sat next to Piper and smiled at her as she flicked open her napkin.

"Starkudos on your mission, Piper," she said.

"Star salutations, Cassie," Piper said, digging into

her bowl of Quasar Krispies with sliced starberries.

"It probably didn't . . ." Cassie said, obviously trying to figure out the best way to phrase her statement. "It probably didn't go quite as seamlessly as mine, did it?" She thought for a moment and laughed, placing a hand on Piper's arm. "Of course it didn't!" she said. "What was I thinking? My mission was such a stellar success!"

Piper looked stricken for a moment. But her expression changed to a knowing grin when she received Astra's holo-text:

 Cassie = Braggy!

The rest of the Star Darlings began to arrive at the table. Astra and Piper watched as Sage giggled when Clover shamefacedly confessed to getting a D on her Chronicle Class examination and then guffawed when the Bot-Bot waiter informed her the kitchen was out of the Sparkle-O's she had ordered.

 Sage = Can't stop laughing.

Piper nodded from across the table and began to write a holo-message in return.

Libby = Can't stay awake.

Astra looked over at the girl, whose cheek was resting on her plate of tinsel toast. *My stars*, she thought. She reached for her mug, drank her last gulp of twinkle tea, and began to compose a reply.

"Hey," said Cassie, noticing. "Are you writing a message about me?" she asked eagerly. She looked down at her silver dress and lace tights and smiled. "I did pick a startastically fashionable outfit today, didn't I?"

"You do look nice today," Astra said. To Piper she holo-texted:

 They don't know that they are acting odd, do they?

 Watch this.

"Vega," she said. "Have you noticed that everything you say rhymes?"

Ten Star Darlings' heads swiveled around to look at Piper, curious looks on their faces.

Cassie cocked her head to the side. "Really?" she said. "I don't hear it."

Gemma turned to Tessa. "Imagine if I talked in

rhyme all the time? That would be so annoying!"

Tessa laughed. "My stars!" she said to her sister. "Bite your tongue!"

"Ouch!" said Gemma.

Vega stared at Piper like she had three auras. "Piper, do you need some schooling? Talking in rhyme? You must be fooling!"

With a quick glance at Astra, Piper asked, "You really didn't just hear that?"

"I think it is completely clear," Vega replied. "There isn't anything to hear."

 Does that answer your question?

 It certainly does!